PARTITA

PARTITA

a novel in linked short stories

BY KRISTINA BAER

PARK PLACE PUBLICATIONS
PACIFIC GROVE, CA

Park Place Publications
P.O. Box 722
Pacific Grove, CA 93950
www.parkplacepublications.com

FIRST EDITION June 2022
PRINT   ISBN – 13: 978-1-953120-51-9
EBOOK ISBN – 13: 978-1-953120-52-6

Second Printing October 2022

Distributed by Ingram Books
Cover Image by Howard Jones
Printed in the United States of America

For Carla
In Memoriam

CONTENTS

Prelude

April 10, 1962

Blindfolded, sitting on the chair just inside the studio door, I hear the closet door across the room open and close and the *shhhh, shhhh, shhhh,* of footsteps coming toward me.

"Mama?"

"I'm here, sweetheart."

Mama unties the blindfold. In front of me, my gold satin cape draped over her right arm, she holds a box wrapped in glossy white paper, a green satin ribbon tied around it.

Smiling, she sets the box in my lap. "Happy birthday, Grace."

I untie the ribbon, remove the wrapping paper. Inside the box, in a nest of white tissue paper, are two pink ballet slippers, sole to sole, heel to toe, toe to heel. They smell like the sea.

"They're made of kidskin," Mama tells me.

Kiss-skin? I imagine the slippers kissing my feet, my feet kissing the carpet.

I slide the slippers on, stretching and smoothing the elastics over my feet. Mama helps me up, slips the satin cape around my shoulders and fastens the snaps under my chin. She gathers my hair in a ponytail and clips the barrette low and snug against the back of my neck.

In the new slippers, my feet seem narrower and longer. I slide my heels together in first position, round my arms, close my eyes, and do a plié.

Mama claps.

She raises her arms over her head, then drops them, shaking her hands. She takes my right hand and holds my palm against her belly, where I can feel the taps. "This baby is a dancer, like you," she says. She laughs, softly. "Or maybe a soccer player." She frowns, hunches her shoulders. Her breath catches.

She closes her eyes. Opens them. "Let's get started, shall we?"

○ ○ ○

In the middle of the studio, Mama's piano is an ebony island surrounded by a sea of blue carpet. Every day she removes its felt cover, folds it, and lays it on the floor underneath the piano. I often curl up on it, eyes closed, while she practices. There, I imagine I'm in a dark, warm cave on Neverland. Outside the cave, birds and animals roam the island, calling to one another in trills, ripples, snorts, and rumbles. The animals leap and bound, the birds soar. One very large animal—at least as big as an elephant, a heffalump, perhaps—sometimes stomps past, gurgling and snuffling.

This morning, the studio's French doors are ajar. The pale blue drapes flutter in the crosscurrents. Just across the patio, the lilac's new leaves shimmer in the low morning light.

"What shall I play for you today, Grace?"

"Day-bussy," I tell her.

"'Deh-byoo-see.'" She pronounces it slowly and carefully as she smooths my hair, centers the ponytail between my shoulders. "Claude Debussy. Can you say that?"

I repeat, softly, barely above a whisper, "Claude Debussy."

"Just right," Mama smiles.

Sitting on the piano bench, she opens the sheet music. The cover is faded blue, the paper pale yellow. Her hands on the keyboard, she murmurs, "We're in the garden. The full moon is rising. The rain has stopped. Waterdrops fall from the leaves into the garden pool. In the moonlight, they look like beads of gold."

Head bowed, eyes closed, she begins to play "Claire de Lune."

Raising and lowering my arms, I turn and tiptoe toward the open doors and the garden. The new slippers cling to the carpet. The cape whispers and flows around me, glimmering in the soft morning light.

I am a bead of gold. I am five years old today.

Mama

1965-1969

When Mrs. Cullen came to work for us in 1965, when Mama first went to the clinic, I was eight. Lil was three. Every Wednesday, she baked. Sometimes she let Lil and me help her make Irish soda bread, Papa's favorite. She gave us each a ball of dough. I watched and imitated her pats, pulls, and taps, the way she stuck her lower lip out to blow wisps of hair away from her face. Lil gobbled raisins and bits of dough until nothing remained of her share but crumbs and her own floury fingerprints, ghostly traces of the deed.

"What a little monkey you are, Miss Lil." Mrs. Cullen scooped her up and held her over the kitchen sink while she washed her hands and face.

On days when Mama came home from the clinic, she lay in bed, a lavender compress over her eyes. Mrs. Cullen sat with us at lunch and told us stories about Ireland and leprechauns "no bigger than you, Miss Lil. Full of tricks, too. That's why you should always mind your manners." Mrs. Cullen gave Lil a look, as if working out how best to make her point. "They watch us, you know."

"Like Santa Claus?"

"Just like Santa Claus."

Lil slumped back in her chair, pouting. "Who cares about lumps of coal?"

Mrs. Cullen nodded. "The leprechauns steal things. They could take Little Blue and hide him." Lil's eyes widened. Little Blue, her blue teddy bear, a gift from Mama, was her favorite.

"Hide him where?"

"In their burrow. That's where leprechauns live, underground."

Lil got down from her chair. She tugged my arm. "Let's go see."

Out in the garden, we poked the hoe handle into the soil, under and around Mama's irises and the forsythia bushes, along the fence and behind the maple tree.

"Where are they, Gracie?"

"Maybe they're on vacation."

Lil dropped the hoe. "She's just talking."

o o o

Sometimes, as she ironed, her voice soft and solemn, Mrs. Cullen told us stories about the life and suffering of "our Lord, Jesus Christ, and the Holy Virgin, his mother Mary." Her voice low, she told us always to remember how much Jesus loved us, how much he had suffered to save us.

"Save us from what, Mrs. Cullen?" Lil wanted to know.

"From burning in Hell, of course." She pursed her lips and shook her head. Lil and I didn't go to church.

"So even if we're naughty, Jesus won't let us go to Hell?"

"Only if you repent."

"What's 'repent'?"

"You have to say you're sorry." Mrs. Cullen made the sign of the cross and patted the silver crucifix she wore on the chain around her neck. "Then, when you die, He'll send his messenger angels and they'll carry you up through the clouds, past the Milky Way, to meet St. Peter, who'll check his book. It's like a phone book, with names and addresses and a list of all the good things you've done, you see. The bad things, too. And it says whether you've done your penance for those. He and Jesus go over that book every day. They know who's coming and when. And if your name is there, why, he'll let you right into the garden. Jesus will be expecting you, of course, so you'll get to have a visit with him. And with Mary, too."

"Hear that, Lil? So when you say 'sorry,' you have to mean it."

Lil stuck out her tongue.

Mrs. Cullen put the iron down. "That's enough now. You girls fold the napkins while I hang your papa's shirts."

I asked Papa. He didn't believe in God or Jesus, heaven or hell, he told me. "I believe every person should try to be and do good in this life."

"Lil doesn't."

"Lil will learn, Grace."

The next morning, Papa didn't go to work. When Mrs. Cullen arrived, he called her into his study and closed the door. Lil and I sat on the landing, listening. I caught bits and pieces: "nonsense," "too young," and "not our way." No shouting, no slammed doors, just the quiet murmur of Papa's voice. Mrs. Cullen came out, her face as red as if she'd been baking. Dabbing her eyes with the hem of her apron, she went back into the kitchen and closed the door.

There were no more stories about Jesus. Or leprechauns. Just reminders to behave, or, "I'll tell your papa."

o o o

One Saturday in June, Mama took the bus home from the clinic. Barefoot, in a blouse and a wraparound skirt, she later told us she'd had to borrow money from the bus driver to pay the fare.

"Grace? Lil? Mrs. Cullen? I'm home!"

Lil and I were in the kitchen with Mrs. Cullen.

Mrs. Cullen called Papa.

Mama sat on the sofa between Lil and me, her bare feet tucked under her. Her braid had come undone. Limp and dull, her hair lay on her shoulders. The sofa's green cover prickled the backs of my legs. Lil squirmed.

Papa came in and sat across from us in the armchair, hands folded in his lap, lips pressed together in a smile that didn't reach his eyes. "They thought you were lost, Elizabeth." His smile faded. "Imagine that."

"Lost? No, dear, I knew exactly where I was going." She looked down at us. "I even knew which bus to take," Mama laughed—she laughed and laughed, until she slumped against the sofa, her face slack and pale, her eyes closed. "I'm so tired, Henry."

Papa helped her stand. She seemed to collapse into herself, a shapeless sack draped over his arm, moving slowly down the hall.

Lil leaned against me. "What's wrong with Mama, Gracie?"

I turned my head so that she couldn't see my tears. "She's just tired from the bus ride. She'll be better after a nap."

○ ○ ○

The next morning, we walked to the park. When we reached the rose garden, Mama stopped. "You go ahead, now. I'll be fine here." We walked a little further. Papa stopped beside a tree to watch Mama.

Eyes closed, standing motionless in the middle of the blooming Peace roses, Mama smiled. In her blue shirtwaist and straw garden hat, she was as pale as the early sunlight that pooled in the rose leaves and blooms. A bee hovered over her shoulder. She opened her eyes. When she lifted her hand, it landed in her palm. She laughed and waved it away.

Mama soon caught up with us, a bouquet of roses cradled in her arms, the stems ragged, her hands and arms dotted with thorns, bloody from scratches.

"You're not supposed to pick them, Mama. It says so over there." Lil pointed at the sign at the edge of the rose bed.

Mama laughed. She stood still while Papa dabbed at her scratches with his handkerchief.

Mama always did something unexpected when we went out with her, like the time she went over to a man sitting on a bench, legs stretched out, barefoot, and told him he had beautiful toes. The man laughed. Papa smiled and shrugged.

Mama was so beautiful. She could say or do anything she pleased.

As soon as we got home, I went to the cupboard in the pantry and took down Mama's favorite crystal vase. Papa trimmed the stems and Mama arranged the blooms, sniffing each one as she placed it with the others. "Heaven. This is how heaven smells."

Papa fumbled for his handkerchief, patted his eyes, ignoring the bloodstains.

o o o

The next day, Papa, Lil, and I went with Mama to Jillian's, the hair salon on Main Street. With its white-and-black tile floor, pink walls, and ruffled white curtains, it looked like a box of Good & Plenty candies, but it smelled of lotions, shampoos, ammonia, and cigarettes, smells that prickled my nose and made my eyes burn.

Mama sat in the chair. Wearing a pink smock, Jillian adjusted the height. She smoothed a white drape around Mama's shoulders, took the hairpins from her braid, and uncoiled it. "You have such beautiful hair, madam. You're sure?"

Mama looked into the mirror, into Papa's eyes. I held my breath. Mama nodded. Papa turned away.

Jillian gripped the braid in her left hand, lifting it away from the back of Mama's neck. It was so quiet I could hear Papa breathing. *Snick! Snick! Snick!* Papa shuddered.

The braid hung limp in Jillian's hand, its end brushing the floor. Sitting in Papa's lap, Lil hid her face against his shoulder.

After washing and drying Mama's hair, Jillian trimmed the rough ends and set it, telling Mama about an actress who had the same style. "So chic, this chin-length bob." Looking at Mama in the mirror as she worked, she nodded and smiled. "It makes you look ten years younger."

Ten years younger? I couldn't tell. Twenty-three in 1947, the year she and Papa married, she would have been thirty-three in 1957, when I was born. She had worn her hair in a braid, wrapped around her head for as long as I could remember. Now, parted on the left, her hair fell in a smooth curve that crossed her forehead, left to right, like a curtain opening—or closing. Papa stared at her, as if she were a stranger. Absorbed in flipping through a magazine, sitting on the other side of Papa, Lil didn't look up.

"This will be easier for you, madam, you'll see."

Jillian wrapped the braid in pink tissue paper and placed it in a black paper bag lettered, in pink cursive, "Hair by Jillian."

In April of the previous year, on my tenth birthday, Mama came home from the clinic.

"Only for the day, girls. Mama is very tired," Papa told us.

Over time, the gaps between these weekend visits had lengthened from days to weeks. Always, as soon as Mama arrived, I became impatient for her to go away again, to get her going-away-again over with. Every time, after a quiet hour with her, sitting beside her on the sofa, talking about school and our friends, Lil squirmed away and ran out of the house. I stayed. We didn't talk. I could hear the clock ticking, as the minutes passed, as I waited for her to leave.

o o o

The day of my twelfth birthday, sitting on the top front step, Lil and I watched for Papa's car. After parking next to the curb, Papa came around to help Mama. Lil started down the steps. Papa shook his head. I grabbed her arm. She yelped.

Mama removed a Macy's shopping bag from the backseat and lifted it high, "Loot," she said, smiling up at us. Papa's arm around her waist, she took the steps one at a time, planting her feet side by side before stepping up to the next one. Panting lightly, she kissed my cheek, her lips cool and soft. Lil reached for her, both arms around her waist. "Mama?"

Papa patted Lil's head. "Let Mama get settled first." Papa guided Mama into the front hall, took her hat and sunglasses, placed them on the console. He reached out to take the bag from her.

"Thank you, Henry. I can manage." She lifted her head, took a deep breath. "Smells like home." Earlier, Mrs. Cullen had dusted and polished the mahogany banister. The smell of beeswax filled the house. Now, it blended with l'Heure Bleue, and the scent of the tomato soup Mrs. Cullen had left warming on the stove an hour earlier.

The grandfather clock on the landing began to strike noon. Mama had had it since she was a little girl. A man had come the day before to clean and wind it.

Holding Lil's hand, Papa followed Mama into the dining room.

I had set the table, spreading and smoothing the white linen tablecloth over the sides and ends of the table; folding the napkins; centering each blue-and-white plate according to Mrs. Cullen's instructions. The silver place settings gleamed; the cut crystal water glasses cast tiny rainbows onto the tablecloth. With Mrs. Cullen's help, I had made the centerpiece—hyacinths, daffodils, and tulips.

I squinted against the bright light. Mama, Lil, and Papa disappeared into the blur of color—Mama's pink dress, Lil's yellow playsuit, and Papa's blue jacket.

Without waiting for us to sit at the table, Mama lifted a box from the shopping bag and handed it to me, smiling. "Happy birthday, darling Grace."

I removed the lid and found a Tiny Tears doll dressed in a pink dress, white socks, white shoes, lying on its back in the tissue paper.

"Mama...."

Mama looked at Papa, uncertain.

"Let me see, Grace." Lil pushed me away to look in the box. "You're too old for a baby doll," she sniffed.

"That'll do, Lil." Papa lifted her onto her chair.

Still holding the Macy's bag, Mama sighed. "Such a pretty day."

"Let's have some lunch, shall we?" Papa took Mama's arm, guiding her to her chair.

On my ninth birthday, I'd asked for a Tiny Tears doll. Then, Mama told me I was too old to play with dolls. She had given me a white angora sweater and a navy-blue pleated skirt.

Like a snapped rubber band, the pressure in my chest released. I ran out of the dining room, out the front door, down the street toward the park. Our front door slammed. "Grace! Come back!" Papa ran down the steps after me.

I ran past the Joneses' house on the corner of Willow Street, where their collie, lying in the sun on the front porch, woofed and wagged her tail. A car drew alongside me and slowed. "Where's the fire, Grace?" Mrs. Jones called. I waved and kept going. The entrance to the park was just ahead. When I looked back, Papa had disappeared.

In the park, I turned off the main, paved sidewalk and headed toward the lake on the footpath. Pines, magnolias, and lilacs lined the footpath; birds called to one another over my head. I stumbled over a root and slowed to a walk.

A pair of mallards, their five ducklings bobbing behind them, paddled by. A bullfrog piped up; a dragonfly skimmed the water. Swallows swooped low, scooping up flies and mosquitoes.

Nearly there.

o o o

Papa and I had discovered the bench. At the edge of a marshy inlet it looked out into a cluster of cattails, hidden from the footpath by a stand of rhododendrons. The first time, we sat in silence, watching the lake, the reflection of passing clouds, the ripples moving with the breeze. I returned, often by myself. Being alone there helped me miss

Mama less, helped me accept her absence. I didn't know what was wrong with her. And no one seemed to know when she would get better.

"Grace?"

Papa came toward me, around the bend, just beyond the inlet.

"Come sit with me." He gave me his handkerchief.

Papa gazed out across the lake, toward the far shore. He put his arm around my shoulders, pulled me close. I wiped my face and handed the handkerchief back to him.

"Mama's being away so much, Mama's being so sick, it's hard." He twisted around so he could look into my eyes. "She has an illness that can't be cured, Grace."

"Ever?"

"Someday maybe someone will find a cure. Until then, we can visit her at the clinic and bring her home when she's well enough."

"Does it have a name?"

"It's called 'depression', Grace, chronic depression."

"How did she catch it?"

Papa looked down at the tear-stained handkerchief, twisted into a knot. He cleared his throat and shook his head. "It's not contagious, Grace. It's not like measles." He shifted around to look at me. "Do you remember after Lil was born, when Mama stopped playing the piano?"

At first, I had thought Mama was too tired, that once she was rested, she'd start again.

Papa blew his nose. "That's when it started. She got lost somewhere, Grace, somewhere in her mind, you could say. I used to think she just forgot how to find her way back. Now, I don't know if she wants to remember."

I leaned my head against Papa's shoulder. When I closed my eyes against the sun's glare, I saw a black, shapeless hole.

○ ○ ○

Two weeks later, we had Friday off from school. It was the longest Mama had been home that I could remember. Lying in her bed during that time, the curtains drawn, she slept, mostly— "just napping," she told Lil and me when we came to see her—or propped herself against the headboard to listen to our stories about school, our friends. We took turns carrying her tray to her, keeping her company while she ate a spoonful of soup or scrambled eggs and sipped her tea. Chamomile tea.

Friends had invited Lil and me to go to the park that Friday. It was a school holiday. At the kitchen table having breakfast, Lil slurped and giggled. I ignored her. Papa came out to the kitchen, tie askew, shirt rumpled.

"Mama's going away today, girls. You two stay home with Mrs. Cullen." He looked over our heads, out the window. Opened his mouth. Closed it.

"But I want to go to the park," Lil whimpered.

"Another time, Lil." He looked at me.

"I'll pack, Papa." I always packed for Mama, and always folded her laundry, changed her sheets, and straightened her room during and after her visits. It never occurred to me to ask Mrs. Cullen to do these chores, or to ask Lil to help me.

At ten, the familiar maroon Buick pulled up. The driver got out and removed a collapsible wheelchair from the trunk. A nurse helped him set it up. He pushed it up the walk. At the foot of the steps, he turned it around and together they pulled it up the steps to the verandah, where Papa waited.

The nurse pushed it toward Mama's room. One of the wheels squeaked. The driver waited on the verandah.

Sitting beside Lil on the bottom stair, I imagined the nurse helping Mama into the wheelchair, smoothing the blanket over her knees, and checking everything I had packed: nightgowns, robe, slippers, underwear, the travel bag that held her medicines and her perfume.

The wheelchair came back down the hall, slower and heavier this time. The squeak had stopped. Dressed in her blue shirtwaist, Mama buried her face in the pillow she held tight to her chest.

Lil sat beside me, biting her nails. Papa stood behind the wheelchair, staring at the floor. In the kitchen, Mrs. Cullen opened and closed cupboards, preparing our lunch.

I grabbed Lil's hand. At the front door, Mama lifted her head, smiled at us. "I'll be back soon." She beckoned to me. I knelt beside her. "Help Papa and Mrs. Cullen, Grace darling."

"Yes, Mama."

"And take care of Lil."

"Yes, Mama."

"Promise?"

"I promise, Mama."

Lil came around me and leaned against the wheelchair. "And me, Mama? What about me?"

Mama smiled. "Listen to Grace. She knows what to do."

The nurse caught Papa's eye. "Everything will be fine, Elizabeth," he said.

The driver put Mama's overnight bag in the trunk. He came back up the steps into the front hall, where the nurse was waiting with Mama. He and the nurse lifted the wheelchair over the threshold and set it down on the verandah. He stepped down to the third step and turned to face Mama and the nurse. The nurse pushed the wheelchair up to the edge of the top step. His back to the car, the driver grasped both sides of the footrest and looked up at the nurse and Mama.

"All set?"

"All set," the nurse replied, holding both sides of the chair.

"One, two, *three*."

On "three" they lifted the chair and Mama and moved it, step by step, to the front walk.

"Did we miss any?" the driver asked, grinning.

"Any what?" Mama asked.

"Any steps." He smiled.

Mama hunched her shoulders and turned away.

Papa went down the steps to the car and helped the nurse settle Mama in the backseat. He crouched beside the open door, took her hand, and spoke to her. All I heard was the word "soon."

As the Buick turned the corner, the grandfather clock chimed ten o'clock.

Lil ran up the stairs, giggling. "Bet you can't find me."

March 12, 1969

Most mornings, I find Papa dozing in the armchair in his study, files and books heaped around him on the floor, his tie loosened, his shirt collar unbuttoned, a throw draped over his knees. Most mornings, Lil complains—about the clothes I laid out for her the night before, about the teacher who makes her do her work over—"sloppy!" Today, she'll fuss about the sleet and the wind. Will she pester Papa for a ride to school?

I turn on the percolator and set out placemats, bowls, spoons, napkins, milk, and cereal: Frosted Flakes for Lil, Wheaties for me. Papa has breakfast at a diner near his office. Sometimes he sits and drinks a cup of coffee with us, the newspaper spread out on the table in front of him.

The blue plastic placemats are faded, their scalloped edges chipped. Mrs. Cullen washes and dries them twice a week. Their smell of Clorox mixes with the aroma of percolating coffee and the dusty odor of heat rising from the radiator. Once, Mama's perfume and her hug greeted us each morning.

Upstairs, Lil dances. The ceiling throbs. For her birthday she bought "Pink Shoelaces," a 45, actual pink shoelaces and dyed her sneakers tan in a pail of tea. (Mrs. Cullen helped.) The purple ribbon from her Easter basket transformed a bedraggled cowboy hat into a "Big Panama with a purple hat band." She made up her own dance steps.

"Why 'Pink Shoelaces'? That song's older than you are."

"You won't get it."

"Try me."

"When I'm twelve, I'm going to have a boyfriend just like Dooley."

"I'm twelve. I don't have a boyfriend."

"I'm not you."

On Lil's last report card, her teacher checked, "Lacks self-control." Papa signed and handed it to her, without comment.

The kitchen's fluorescent lights buzz. In their yellow glare the wallpaper's blue morning glories fade to muddy green. There's a brown smear of dried glue where Lil tore off a piece of wallpaper next to her place at the end of the kitchen table.

o o o

The phone rings.

The extension phone hangs on the wall next to the refrigerator.

"Hello?" Papa answers the phone in his study.

I slide my hand over the mouthpiece and lift the kitchen phone receiver, slowly.

"She's gone, sir," a woman says.

"What?" Papa's voice is hoarse, the way it is sometimes when I interrupt him, when he stays up late, working at home. He coughs, then clears his throat.

"I'm so sorry," the woman says.

Papa starts to speak. He coughs, clears his throat again. "When?"

"At four past six this morning, sir."

Mama's grandfather clock in the front hallway begins to strike seven.

Upstairs, Lil shoves her bed across the floor, bangs a drawer shut. Papa hangs up. I hang up.

Carrying his hat and overcoat, Papa comes out to the kitchen, shoulders slumped, his mouth set in a hard, thin line.

"You heard?"

I nod, waiting for him to scold me.

He drapes his coat over his chair and pours a cup of coffee. One of the ceiling lights flickers and goes out. In the gloom, the morning glory leaves in the wallpaper appear wrinkled and brown, withered. The kitchen sink—white, like the refrigerator—is yellowed, soiled-looking. I look down at the grey linoleum floor, at the narrow band of darkness between my feet and the linoleum. I'm sinking into my shadow.

Lil comes into the kitchen, drops her sneakers with the pink shoelaces on the floor beside her chair, sits, pours milk onto her cereal, and stirs it, faster and faster, until milk and Frosted Flakes spill onto the table.

"Stop it." I reach across the table to blot the spill with a paper napkin.

"Say 'please.'" She waits, grinning, swinging her legs back and forth, bumping the table.

I put my dish in the sink. Lil stares at Papa sitting at the end of the table, head bowed, shoulders rigid, gripping his coffee mug in both hands as if clinging to life itself. "What's wrong, Papa?"

Papa doesn't answer, doesn't look up.

Lil shrugs. She lifts her bowl and slurps. Eyeing us, she slides off her chair. "Will you take me to school, Papa?"

"Not today."

"But it's raining."

He closes his eyes, shakes his head. "Not today, Lil." This time, his voice, his lawyer voice, is flat, calm, final. He clears his throat and swallows some coffee.

Lil finishes her cereal and leaves us, sticking her tongue out as she turns the corner into the hallway.

"Did Mama take the bus by herself, like the last time, Papa?" I ask.

He reaches for the milk-soaked napkin. The sudden move jars the table. "What last time?" A gust of wind shakes the house. TV laughter and music rise and fall in the den down the hall next to Papa's study. Papa holds the napkin in both hands, squeezing it. Milk drips onto the tabletop.

"Like she did that time in the summer, when she took the bus, remember?"

Papa shakes his head. "No."

"But the lady said …."

"Grace…." He lets out a rough, deep breath, a breath that trails off into a hoarse sigh. A groan. "Grace," he says again. "What she said …." He opens his hands, staring down at the soggy napkin, as if he has no idea where it came from or what it is.

"I heard her, Papa."

He breathes out, clears his throat. "What you heard, Grace…." He looks down at his cup of coffee. "What she said …," He looks at me. "Mama died, Grace. She died this morning at four minutes past six."

"But what about what the lady said? She said Mama was gone."

He shakes his head. "Later, Grace."

Papa stands and puts on his hat and overcoat. "You and Lil stay home today. Tell Mrs. Cullen I'll be at the clinic. I'll be back for lunch." In the doorway, he turns. "Sometimes, when people have bad news, they're afraid to say what they mean. Like the lady on the phone. She said Mama's gone …." He rubs his eyes, looks at me. "What she meant …. What she meant is, Mama died, Grace. Mama is dead."

I look at the clock. It's 7:10. Mama died at four minutes past six, one hour and six minutes ago.

One time, Mama made me eat mashed turnips. I stuffed my

mouth so full I gagged when I tried to swallow, choking on the bits that stuck in my throat. Then, I couldn't breathe. Now, I can't speak or swallow past the lump in my throat, can't tell Papa he hasn't shaved or combed his hair. Or that his hat is on backwards. Or remind him Mrs. Cullen has the day off.

Maybe I'll never speak again.

On the wall calendar next to the kitchen phone, today's date, March 12, is circled in black with a note in Papa's handwriting: "Lil. Orthodontist."

Years later, I will remember this day as the day we canceled Lil's appointment with the orthodontist because Mama died.

○ ○ ○

Did Mama know it was Wednesday, March 12? Did she know it was "raining to beat the band," as Mrs. Cullen liked to say?

Sitting at the kitchen table after school one day, I'd been telling Mama a story Mrs. Cullen had told me about her own father, who had been born in Ireland, the only member of her family to have kissed the Blarney Stone—which she hoped to do someday.

"Just remember you can't always believe what Mrs. Cullen tells you," Mama said.

"Mrs. Cullen lies?"

Mama laughed. "I mean she likes to tell stories. And she wants you to like her." She reached up to straighten the collar of her cashmere sweater, one of my favorites because its blue made her eyes seem bluer still, blue as a clear summer sky. She had been home from the clinic for a week.

"But doesn't she know it's wrong to tell lies, to make things up?"

Mama laughed again. "Most of Mrs. Cullen's lies are what we call 'white lies'. They can't hurt you. But if you're not sure about something she says, ask Papa. He'll tell you." Mama took me by the shoulders. "Be very kind to Mrs. Cullen, Grace, she has had a hard life."

"How?"

"Well, she's Irish. She never went to school, you know." Mama frowned. "That doesn't mean she isn't a good person, Grace. Her beliefs may be different from ours, but we can't manage without her." She looked away, out the window, and sighed, embarrassed or relieved—or, maybe, both. "Just remember you can't believe everything she says."

o o o

Is dying like walking through a doorway, then closing the door behind you?

Does Mama know she's dead?

o o o

I fold back the bedspread, get into Mama's bed and pull the sheet over me. I bury my face in the pillow, which smells of l'Heure Bleue—l'Heure Bleue, the blue hour, the hour just before dawn, the hour just after sunset, pale blue like the drapes in Mama's studio, like her cashmere sweater. The mirror above the dressing table reflects the light from the door, ajar, across the room. Lil's laughter carries over the sound of the TV.

I get up and sit at the dressing table, my feet resting on the crossbar. Grown-ups tell me I look like Mama. My face is heart-shaped like hers, but I have Papa's brown hair, his nose, and his brown eyes. Lil's hair is reddish blond like Mama's, and her eyes are blue-grey, just like Mama's.

Framed photographs line up, side by side along the back of the dressing table: Mama, fourteen, squints into the sun, bareback on her mare, Dolly; Mama and Papa on their wedding day, Mama's lace veil draped around her shoulders, falling in a cascade of folds and ripples to the floor, her white gown flaring from her waist, her hand through Papa's arm. Head turned toward her, he smiles. She smiles into the camera. Me, age five, sitting in Mama's yellow armchair and holding Lil, one, in my lap.

In the last photo, hands positioned on the keyboard, Mama sits at the piano in her blue velvet gown, a white orchid gleaming on her right shoulder.

Mama's ivory brush, comb, and silver-backed hand mirror lie on the table below the mirror. Next to them, the Blue Willow candy dish holds her rings, the pearl earrings Papa gave her on their engagement, a gold bangle, and a handkerchief embroidered with her initials. The bottle of l'Heure Bleue sits at the far end of the table.

I lift the bottle, close my eyes, tilt my head to the left, and depress the button, the way Mama does—*the way Mama did*—shivering at the spray's cool prickle against my neck. Opening my eyes, turning my head, I hold the hand mirror and examine my profile in the dressing table mirror. Papa's eyes, Papa's nose. The musky scent of the brush bristles mingles with the odor of Mama's hair, the lavender fragrance of her shampoo, and the breath of l'Heure Bleue wafting around me.

I set the mirror down, open the bottom drawer, and remove the shoebox. The lid isn't sealed. Inside, wrapped in a linen handkerchief, Mama's braid lies on a layer of tissue paper. It smells of l'Heure Bleue and a dark, stale scent I can't identify.

I uncoil and drape it over my shoulder so that it hangs over my chest, to my waist. When I look in the mirror, I see Mama—Mama's eyes looking back at me.

Grace
1981-1994

March 1981

"Swallow a canary?" Matt smiles.

"At least one. Maybe six," I gloat. I've read enough to know that one night of sleep at this stage is no guarantee.

Matt kisses my cheek, nuzzles my neck. "You should both be proud of yourselves."

"Wait. There's more." I guide his hand, placing it on my belly so he can feel the flutters.

"Swimmer or place kicker?"

"He—"

"Or she—"

"—can be or do whatever, wherever, as long as I can sleep."

"I thought of another name." Matt lies back, hands folded on his chest.

"Me, too. Tell me yours?"

We play our name game first thing in the morning—boys against girls. So far, on our list of forty-three names, boys are ahead by one.

"This name swings both ways."

"So it'll only even things out if we add it to the girls' side."

Matt rolls onto his side, leans on his elbow and looks down at me.

"Or we could add it to both lists?"

"That's cheating." I grin up at him. "Take your pick: will it be boys or girls?"

"Dana," he says. "What do you think of 'Dana'?"

I whisper it, then say it. "Dana. Someone you know?"

"A girl, third grade."

"Let me guess. She beat you at checkers?"

Matt laughs. "She could pitch and dribble as well as any boy. Whenever I got to be captain, she was my first pick."

"What happened?"

"She only had eyes for Jack, my best friend."

"Your first crush?"

Matt mock pouts. "Jack married her."

"Well, there you go." Now the kicking is stronger. I prop myself up on my elbows. "I like it. Girls' side keeps it."

Matt's mother, Dorothy, had been nicknamed "Dotty." Not "Dorothy," we agreed.

"What about a middle name? What about Elizabeth?"

"Dana Elizabeth Carlson." I said it aloud. "'Dana Elizabeth Carlson. Come here right now.' That should get her attention, don't you think?" Matt grinned. "So far, that's my first choice. If she's a 'she', that is."

"And if she's a 'he'?"

"Thomas Alexander Carlson." My father's first name was Thomas. Matt's middle name was Alexander.

Matt nodded. "I think we're done, don't you?"

"But we've got five months to go."

"Fine with me. We can sleep in. Or I can bring you breakfast in bed."

"Aren't you forgetting something?"

"Like work?"

"Like work. Like time to get up, now."

I nudged him toward the edge of the bed.

o o o

Matt and I had discussed and decided not to name our daughter Elizabeth. Not that I was superstitious, but because calling her 'Elizabeth' would summon the old ghosts, my enduring loss, every time we spoke her name. But giving her Mama's name as her middle name would honor my love for Mama and my earliest memories of our time together. *Before Lil.*

Of course, I wanted our children to know about Mama, to know her story. When they asked about her, I would tell them about her talent and her love of music. Maybe one of them would want to play the piano. How much and when to talk about Mama's illness and death would depend on time and opportunity, which I couldn't predict and wouldn't force.

o o o

At breakfast, Matt repeated "Dana Elizabeth Carlson" several times, stressing "Carlson," like the end of a musical phrase. "That does it all right." He smiled. "It's a fine name for our girl, Grace."

"And Thomas Alexander Carlson?" Matt raised his eyebrows, grinning. I giggled.

"We'll use it for the next one, assuming our girl comes first."

"Or vice versa?"

"No wonder you're a lawyer."

o o o

Like several friends, I've suffered off and on from PMS. Always, I've made light of it in public, as they do. I stifle my apprehension in the hope that if I don't talk about Mama's condition and her death, I'll be safe.

When I learned I was pregnant, of course I told my doctor about Mama. "It's normal to experience mood swings after the baby is born, Grace. But we don't know if post-partum depression is hereditary. Given your mother's history, we'll keep an eye on how you're feeling." He took off his glasses, wiped them, put them back on, and continued. "We know even less about the causes of chronic depression." His bristly eyebrows curled over the tops of his rimless glasses like awning fringes. When he smiled, they lifted slightly. "One step at a time, Grace. Try to relax. And remember: You are not your mother."

Every morning after that appointment, I stood in the bathroom, looking into my eyes in the mirror, repeating "I am not Mama."

o o o

My friend, Ellen, who had two children, advised me to learn to cat-nap. "Get ahead of the curve now, Grace, and the first year will be a walk in the park." She grinned. "Easier, at least."

At 5:00 a.m. on June 30, 1981, a week after my due date, a strange sound woke me.

"What's that noise?"

"What noise?" Matt sat up next to me, looking around, as if whatever was making the sound had to be hidden somewhere in the room.

"Humming," I said.

"I don't hear it."

I covered my ears. I could still hear it. I uncovered my ears. "Seems to be coming from me." A twinge rippled through me.

I made it to the bathroom before the next one, repeating to myself, "I am not Mama."

Throughout the delivery, Matt talked to me, breathed with me, slipped ice chips into my mouth. Afterward, I remembered very little: the humming sound I'd heard that morning; Matt timing the contractions; the doctor's assurance that everything was just fine; and Dana, her mouth wide open, announcing her arrival, greeting her new world.

I held her close, whispering, "Welcome to life, Dana Elizabeth, welcome home."

o o o

During our first weeks, Dana and I recovered quickly. She learned how to sleep. I continued to catnap. Engrossed in her every move, even when she was asleep, or reading books about every imaginable feature of child development, I didn't worry that I might, like Mama, suffer from depression later on. I missed her intensely. I wanted her to know me now, to know Dana. And I knew that I wanted to tell Dana about her, that I would plan how to tell her, that we would go through Mama's story together. Maybe by sharing it with Dana, my sense of loss would soften and, eventually, disappear.

Nursing Dana one afternoon when she was six months old, I closed my eyes, drifting into a revery. As if Mama were sitting beside me, I heard her say, "Take care of Lil, Grace. Promise me you'll take care of Lil."

Lil.

My chest tightened in fear. I wanted to run away, to hide, to escape my fear, and my anger, as I had on my birthday, twelve years ago.

When she left us for the last time, of course I promised Mama I would take care of Lil. Without knowing what was wrong with her, without knowing that she would never come home again, how could I have said no? I never asked who would take care of me. I never asked why she couldn't take care of us herself.

I had done my best to fulfill my promise.

I whispered, "Lil is fine, Mama. She is managing on her own. I'm taking care of Dana now." Dana stirred in my arms, murmuring against my breast. She reached for my hand, took hold of my index finger. I remembered sitting beside Mama, holding her hand, as she slept one afternoon when I came into her room after school. She no longer played the piano. She had told me she was too tired to practice.

But she listened to music all day long in her head, she said, playing again the pieces she had known and loved so well.

Lil, Mama. Dana.

Dana was here. Lil was not.

When Matt came home, I told him what I suspected, that a hormone imbalance wasn't the sole cause of Mama's depression.

"What makes you think that?"

"There's so much, Matt, bits and pieces I understand now. For instance, she didn't hold or cuddle Lil much, didn't play the piano for her, the way she did for me. Maybe she would have been all right if I had been an only child. Lil was such a challenge, right from the beginning. Mama didn't know what to do. And because she didn't know what to do, she gave up. After her collapse, she closed herself off from us."

"Even from your father?"

"Even from Papa. And when she was there, I mean at home from the clinic, she wasn't there, you know? It was like living with a ghost."

"So what did she want?"

"A concert career. That's what she trained for. Lil and I weren't part of that picture." Dana lay belly-down on the sofa between us. I clasped Matt's hand in mine, resting on her back. We could feel her breathing. "Before we were born, Mama gave private and public recitals. She even had a few students. After I was born, she took time off from performing, but she continued to practice. Occasionally she played, but only for Papa or for friends. The public recital she planned after Lil was born was supposed to be her comeback."

I sat beside Papa that evening. In her blue velvet gown, her hair gleaming under the spotlights, Mama came out onto the stage, bowed, and went to the piano, a Steinway concert grand. She sat as the hall grew quiet, hands in her lap, her eyes closed.

Papa shifted in his seat, cleared his throat, and leaned forward. People near us looked at one another, waiting. A minute? Two minutes? An eternity, it seemed. At last she began to play the Bach

Partita, the first piece. In the middle, she stopped, and collapsed onto the keyboard.

Matt held me close. "You and Lil weren't responsible, Grace. And your father did the best he could."

"I understand that now. Not then. Then, I was frightened and confused. Mama never played the piano again. I never danced for her again. And Papa withdrew more and more, the longer Mama was sick. Only when I was twelve did he try to explain. And then I promised Mama I'd take care of Lil. The cloud that hung over my childhood— and Lil's, to be fair—just loomed larger, as long as we were at home."

o o o

With Tom and Ben, born two and four years after Dana, I survived the sleepless first four months in anticipation of the last five. And apart from the fatigue following labor—followed by the fatigue of caring for three young children—I escaped my mother's fate. Our children. Our miracles.

Managing my job and the three children when they were young, I discovered energy to spare and a sense of humor. Like a bad dream, the dark days of Lil faded away. The architecture firm where I worked gave me maternity leave, enough time off to recover and organize our family routines. And Matt pitched in. Whenever he could, he brought his cases home, and worked on them through the clutter and the disruptions.

Matt's sense of humor, and his patience, carried us through the usual childhood crises. My organizational skills—knowing who had to be where, when, wearing what—rounded out our talents as parents. I did not push Dana to take charge of her brothers. When she offered to help, I accepted. For one thing, she knew better than I how to distract Tom and channel his abundant energy. For another, she encouraged Ben's interest in plants and drawing.

When Dana was eight, I asked my doctor about the likelihood that she might suffer from depression.

"Don't go looking for trouble, Grace," he laughed. "Besides, by the time Dana is your age, we'll have many options to treat PMS and post-partum depression." He leaned back in his chair, tapping my chart with his pen, as if conjuring these treatments out of thin air. "Anyway, maybe you and Matt broke the spell."

o o o

March 12, 1994

It's like being at the car wash, water jets pummeling the car roof, windshield, and doors. There, the car moves steadily, slowly, away from the din, shedding grimy suds. Here in the kitchen, the wind buffets the roof and chimney, the sleet splatters against the storm windows.

"Winter's last hurrah," the weatherman predicted. Wishful thinking. Here in Middletown, Rhode Island, on Aquidneck Island, winter, like summer, makes its own rules. Spring's start, March 20, is often observed in the breach. Two years ago, a late March blizzard heaped snowdrifts across the island, piling downed trees and clots of wire helter-skelter on streets and main roads.

I've taken the day off. This year, spring cleaning tops my list of chores, starting with the kids' rooms—a task best left for a school day, when they aren't around to defend their turf.

The dishwasher's steady, comforting hum is no match for the battering gusts, a harbinger of worse to come. I carry the vacuum cleaner and a roll of plastic bags upstairs, longing for the convenience of the built-in vacuum system my firm includes in all our new houses. Even Mrs. Cullen would agree. Like the house I grew up in, this house— built by a 19th-century ship's captain—has plenty of room for us and nooks, crannies, and crawl space for all our clutter. And dust mice and spiders.

The wind whistles down the chimney; the house shudders. At the end of the hallway, Dana's door is ajar. There's a note on her bed beside her patent leather pumps: "Mom, please do NOT throw these away—unless you plan to replace them THIS WEEK. St. Patrick's Day dance, remember? Kisses, D."

At thirteen, Dana favors skirts and button-down collar blouses, Shetland sweaters, knee socks and loafers, and taffeta party dresses. This phase will soon end, I believe. I've noticed that her closest friend, Katie, a year older, sticks to jeans and tank tops, or the equivalent, for school. Dana chose and paid for the patent leather pumps herself and has nearly outgrown them. I leave them on the bed. What harm can it do for her to wear them to one more party?

Before I plug in the vacuum, the hallway light flickers, dims, and goes out. The furnace sighs and stops.

No vacuuming today. At least I can pile and sort old clothes, shoes, and other items the kids no longer use or need. Down in the kitchen, I pick up the cardboard boxes stacked in the corner for this purpose. Between the plastic bags and the boxes, I can sort and stash what to toss, and what to donate.

I start with Dana's bookshelf, mostly textbooks she no longer needs or uses. On the top shelf, she keeps her dictionary and her Latin books. (We argued about it, but I convinced her to try it. Last year, she got an A.) The Latin book will go back to the school. I know and cringe at the thought that there are overdue library books here, too. I scrawl: Box number one, books—donations and returns.

I loved Latin—its logic and organization made it fun. Best of all, I didn't have to speak it. Dana enjoyed it for the same reasons. In the half-light, I page through the textbook, surprised how much I remember of the first declension, the "easy" verbs.

o o o

At least once during every Latin class, my seventh-grade teacher, Mrs. Osborne—tiny, rotund, terrifying—found a reason to tell us stories about Julius Caesar. Thirty-one years ago, on March 5, 1963, after teaching us the conjugation of *monere*, "to warn," she told us about Caesar's run-in with the augur on his way to the Forum, about the Ides of March, how Caesar ignored the soothsayer's warning. Hours later, he was assassinated. Mrs. Osborne wrote on the blackboard: "Beware the Ides of March." I wasn't superstitious, but I felt goosebumps, imagining the scene in the Forum.

Every year, the beginning of March summons that lesson, and the phone call from the clinic; the storm; the buzzing, flickering fluorescent light; Papa's expressionless eyes, his stillness; Lil's pink socks; her spilled cereal.

Old habits die hard. No matter that Lil, 32, now takes care of herself. Wherever she is, whatever she's doing, I still worry about her, the same way I worry about Dana, Tom, and Ben.

I used to call her to talk about Mama every year on March 12. Five years ago, she asked me not to. She wanted to remember Mama in her own way, she said. Since then, I call her on her birthday and sometimes at Christmas. But we never speak about Mama. When I told her Matt and I will spend two weeks on the Gaspé peninsula in July this summer, she offered to come out and stay with the kids. Ben, especially, is looking forward to her visit.

"At least all the people I worry about will be in one place for a change," I'd told Matt.

o o o

I carry the box of Dana's castoffs down to the kitchen. Every year there seem to be fewer items to discard. Since Dana's growth spurt is behind her—she's nearly 5'4"—her clothes, at least, last longer now. And if she follows in Katie's footsteps, she'll soon be borrowing clothes from all her friends. She'll double her wardrobe at a third of the cost. Although this is far from a plan to cut back on her clothing allowance, it will work—at least for a couple of years.

Wind gusts shake the remaining slush from the tree branches. A dislodged bird's nest dangles from a branch of the maple outside the kitchen, swinging from side to side. The bird feeder bobs on its pole, scattering sunflower seeds over the delta of melting snow and ice in front of the garage.

Tacked to the bulletin board beside the wall phone, Ben's watercolor of a pink rose in full bloom catches the light. *Think June, Mom,* he had told me.

The kitchen lights flicker once, then remain on. The refrigerator whirrs back to life.

As the dishwasher switches from wash to rinse, the phone rings. Robo-call? Wrong number? Only Matt, the kids, and my office know I've taken the day off. Has something happened at school? I pour the last of the coffee into a clean mug and lift the receiver.

"It's me." Lil.

I reach for a stool and drag it closer to the end of the counter. The stool protests, its unprotected wooden feet streak the tile floor. When the kids do this, I scold them. Their reaction to my heedlessness isn't hard to imagine. Dana would roll her eyes and Tom would tease. Ben would blush and duck his head, embarrassed for me. Yes, the details always matter. Doing things the right way matters. What does Lil want now? That question drowns out the voice telling me to lift, not drag, the stool.

I tuck the phone between my ear and my shoulder and reach for the pitcher of milk.

Just listen, I tell myself. *Hear her out.*

"Are you there, God?"

We both laugh. After Mama died, when Papa closeted himself in his study—or travelled, leaving us in Mrs. Cullen's care—we would sit together under the covers in Mama's bed and read Judy Blume's book aloud to each other.

"God's procrastinating." I take a sip of coffee.

"Work?"

"Worse than."

"And that would be?"

"Spring cleaning."

"I'll have to look that one up in my thesaurus."

A freelance travel writer, Lil is strictly low maintenance. She lives in a studio apartment south of Market Street in San Francisco. "I can't have things, Grace," she used to tell me. "Clutter slows me down. Sometimes I have only an hour to pack and make a flight. And I may be gone for a month. Don't ask how many plants I've killed."

When Matt pointed out that Lil's footloose ways work for her, I reminded him that's because someone else makes her travel arrangements for her, meets her plane, and schedules her interviews. "All she has to do is show up."

Matt smiled, "Green-eyed monster?"

In fact, I don't envy her. Trusting someone else to take care of me is not an option.

To me, the difference between managing (me) and surviving (Lil) is self-evident. Being prepared for the worst makes the worst manageable. In our life together, Matt is amenable; Admiral Grace, Vice-Admiral Matt—these are comfortable roles that we play with ease, roles that balance our marriage. And our parenting. I once overheard Tom tell Ben, "Mom's the boss."

"That's 'cause Dad wants someone else to make the decisions," Ben retorted.

When I told Matt later, he laughed. "Win-win, I'd say, wouldn't you?"

Every day I oversee a team of ten architects and draftsmen, coordinating schedules, projects, and contractors. I learned long ago that

I'm a good manager and problem-solver (the staff has nicknamed me "The Fixer"). I have only myself to blame for Lil's offhand attitude. Until she left for college, I sorted out her life for her. I expected she would learn to manage for herself when she could no longer count on me to step in. Since then, she skims along, winging it until she hits a bump in the road. Was this one of those times?

Hear her out.

I smooth out the strain in my voice with another sip of coffee. "What's up?"

"I've got good-bad news. Or maybe I should say bad-good news?" Her forced laugh fills the lengthening silence at my end. "Aren't you at least curious?"

"Tell me the good news part."

"A peach of an assignment," she crows. "*Travel & Leisure* wants me to do a story about the Cinque Terre. They're sending me for a whole month, which means I'll have a home base, someone to do my laundry, and a driver. Like a real tourist."

Who wouldn't want to spend a month in the Cinque Terre, wined and dined by the latest hot restaurateurs, exploring the villages and markets for unusual bits and pieces—a new olive oil, or wine, perhaps, or an undiscovered potter or painter?

"When?"

"In July. Everything's set. Places to go, people to see, the usual folderol."

July. So that's the bad news part. The plan had been for Lil to spend two weeks in July in Middletown with Dana, Tom, and Ben, while Matt and I are on vacation in the Gaspé.

"They've hired a photographer I've worked with before. That's a huge plus."

"What happened to the other writer?"

"He backed out. Can you imagine?"

"Ben will be disappointed." Ben wanted to show Lil his latest discovery, the old-growth forest in Portsmouth, just five miles from our house.

"I'm sorry, Grace. I'll make it up to him somehow. I promise."

"That's tall order—unless, perhaps, you'd like to take him with you."

Lil laughs. "Maybe another time?"

This isn't the first time that Lil's change of plans has disrupted ours. So far in her life, she seems to believe that everyone is like her—if something comes up, if you must change your plans, do so, and move on. At least I'll have some time to fix this. "I've got three months. I'll figure something out." I'm ready to hang up, but the silence at Lil's end tells me she's not through. "What is it?"

"Mama. It's been twenty-five years. It seems longer, doesn't it?"

"Sometimes." Lil was seven when Mama died. Mama had spent those years in and out of the clinic. What does Lil remember about that time? Growing up, we rarely talked about Mama, as if discussing her death—as if talking about her at all—were somehow taboo. Like the dangling, empty bird's nest in the maple tree outside the kitchen window, holding the shape of last year's nestlings, I often feel Mama's presence. Latin class again. I hear Mrs. Osborne explaining how "immanence" derives from *immanere*, "to remain in place."

The hum of traffic at Lil's end seems louder now, as though she's up, moving around her living room. It's six thirty there. Maybe she has an early appointment?

"Maybe I could stop and stay with you for the weekend on my way back, the first weekend in August?"

The kids had expected her to stay for two weeks, at least. A weekend won't cut it.

"Or the second? My return date is still a bit soft." She pauses. "I'm sorry, Grace. Please tell Ben? Explain about the Cinque Terre?"

"We'll survive. Don't worry." I scribble a note: *Camp for Ben?* "I hope it'll be a good trip for you."

The throb of my pulse drowns out the broken shutter, flinging itself against the front of the house.

o o o

Three years ago, when Lil had been out of college for nearly ten years, moving from place to place, assignment to assignment, I suggested she find a full-time job—as a staff writer, say, or an editor.

"Cooped up with the same people day-in, day-out? Office politics? No thanks," she scoffed.

"At least she knows she's a square peg," Matt said. "She'll do fine on her own."

"On her own with a safety net—me."

"Or someone else?"

"So far, Mr.—or Ms.—Someone Else hasn't shown up for work."

"Just say no?"

"You know I can't, and why."

I'd learned the Girl Scout song about making and keeping promises. Even now, twenty-five years later, I can hear my scout troop singing in unison, hear Mama's voice as she left us the last time,

"Help Papa and Mrs. Cullen, Grace darling."

"Yes, Mama."

"And take care of Lil."

"Yes, Mama."

"Promise?"

"I promise, Mama."

Then, I didn't think about the future, only about not disappointing Mama. Little did I know that the ties that bound me to my promise would have a life of their own, like any other habit, good or bad.

Matt was right about Lil. In her twenties, after college, on her own, she discovered her talent and worked her way into a career as a travel writer. Now, she's made it. I can't blame her for accepting this assignment. I take a mental step back and consider the problem the way I'd consider a scheduling change at work. She's given me plenty of notice, after all.

I'll figure something out. It's what I'm good at, isn't it?

o o o

In 1975, near the end of seventh grade, Lil let her hair grow, parted it in the middle, ironed it straight, and took up graffiti, as did her three best friends. I knew about the graffiti. Papa didn't. When peace symbols and "Make Love Not War" appeared on buildings downtown, an editorial in the *Courier News* urged schools and parents to "teach their children to respect others and their property."

If Papa found out, I warned her, he would send her away. To boarding school. The effect of that threat lasted until Lil and her friends discovered the derelict warehouse in the industrial park at the edge of town. I found her paint-spattered clothes under the bath towels at the bottom of the laundry basket.

"I'll make a deal with you."

Leaning over the bathroom sink, rimming her eyes with black eyeliner, Lil looked at me in the mirror. "What kind of deal?"

"The 'we both win' kind of deal."

She turned around. "I'm listening."

"If you keep your grades up, I won't tell Papa."

Fingering and tossing her hair until it fell over her shoulders, Lil turned around again, eyeing the results in the mirror. She lifted her hair off her neck to the top of her head, then shook it free. "And if we get caught?"

I laughed. "I won't have to tell Papa. Someone else will."

She rolled her eyes.

o o o

An air current curls around my ankles. In the living room, I discover that the flue in the fireplace has dropped open—the ghost, on its way out. Once, I told Lil that these barely-there currents were family ghosts passing through, to reassure us they were with us still.

"Even Mama?"

"Especially Mama."

"I don't believe you."

Of course, I hoped she'd believe me and, believing me, she'd want to please Mama and change her ways.

The week after we made our deal, I found the pouch, tucked between Lil's mattress and headboard when I was changing the sheets. I took it downstairs and emptied the contents on the kitchen table: a lighter and four joints. Throw everything away? Hide the pouch and its contents and threaten to tell Papa? Would that keep her in line?

It was nearly dinnertime when she came home. Rustling noises, the screech of her bed pushed across the floor, rumbled down into the kitchen. She pounded down the stairs two at a time. Eyes lined in kohl, hair ratted and sprayed, wearing a lace, see-through top, jean jacket, thigh-length skirt—all black—and black leather belt fastened with dime-sized grommets, she stood in the doorway to the kitchen, eyeing the pouch and the joints on the table.

Just then, Papa came in the front door, crossed the hallway, and stopped at the foot of the stairs. "Girls?"

"In the kitchen, Papa." Sitting at the table, I waited.

Papa stood behind Lil in the doorway, loosening his tie to reach the top button of his shirt. "What is it now?"

I gestured at the pile on the table.

Papa picked up a joint and sniffed it. "Where'd you get the pot, Lil?"

"Belongs to a friend," Lil muttered.

"I suppose you mean one of those girls who vandalized the warehouse."

So Papa had known all along.

"You'll be sorry." Lil glared at us and ran out of the kitchen and up the stairs. Her door slammed.

Papa took a beer from the refrigerator. "No dinner for me tonight." He picked up the joints, the lighter, and the pouch and went down the hall to his study.

The next morning, Lil didn't come down for breakfast. Papa said, "See what she's up to, please."

I opened the door to her room. The sheets had been stripped from her bed. Her blanket, pillow, and bedspread were folded on the end of the bed. Her schoolbooks and notebook were stacked on her desk. Scrawled on the mirror over her dresser in red lipstick, her message read, "Told you so."

Three days later, she called from the Port Authority Bus Terminal in New York. She'd run out of money. Papa phoned a friend, who met her, bought her a return ticket, and put her on the bus.

o o o

Until I left for college, Papa and I, day by day, survived Lil's disruptions. The year she went to college, he gave up his practice and spent his time writing articles about constitutional law and tending the rose garden he had planted for Mama.

He died of a heart attack on March 19, 1990, a week after the twenty-first anniversary of Mama's death.

Dana
1989-1997

June 30, 1989

Opening and closing cupboards. Tom and Ben in the kitchen, laughing and teasing. The familiar morning fragrance of bacon, brewing coffee, and pancakes—the ordinary sounds and smells of an ordinary school day. Except this was no ordinary day. Today was my birthday.

Below my bedroom window, just beyond the patio, blooming daffodils bobbed in the morning breeze under the dogwood near the front gate. A blue panel truck pulled in and parked in the driveway. Two men dressed in khaki overalls got out.

"Hurry up, Dana," the boys yelled up the stairs.

When I came into the kitchen, they began to giggle.

"What?"

"Not 'sposed to say," Ben muttered.

"Why not?"

"You'll see," Tom said.

"Shush, you two." Mom came out to the kitchen and closed the door to the front hall behind her. With a warning look at Tom and Ben, she served my pancakes and bacon, smiling as she set my plate on the table. "Happy birthday, sweetheart." She kissed the top of my head.

Ben and Tom finished their pancakes. "Can we go now, Mom?" Tom asked.

"When Dana's done." Mom handed a puzzle to Tom, a coloring book and crayons to Ben.

I heard Dad's voice, then the two men talking in the front hall, and wheels rolling across the floor. Maybe they were delivering my birthday present, the bicycle I'd picked out at the bike shop? Maybe the bike came in a crate, and they brought it into the house to unpack? Mom picked up the boys' plates and put them in the dishwasher. Ben looked up from coloring and reached across the table, making an airplane noise, pretending to dive at my plate, fingers outstretched, aiming at my bacon.

"No way. My birthday, my breakfast."

"Well, hurry up," Ben said. "We want to see your special present."

I ate the last bite of pancake and bacon and swallowed the rest of my orange juice. When Mom finished clearing the table, she pulled a scarf from her apron pocket, "First, the blindfold."

"Blindfold?"

"Because this present is too big to wrap."

Mom led me into the living room and removed the blindfold. As soon as my eyes adjusted, I looked around. "What happened to the bike?"

"Bike? What bike?" The boys hooted and laughed.

Every day, on my way home from school, I walked past the bike shop, stopping to see if the green, three-speed Schwinn was still in the window, imagining learning how to use the gears, keeping up with my friends as they raced around our neighborhood, effortlessly climbing the hill to the school, and speeding down the other side. On the bike I'd learned to ride when I was six, I dragged along, barely able to keep my balance on its fat soft tires.

Mom put her hand on my shoulder. "Take another look, Dana." Her voice quavered.

This morning, there was no green three-speed Schwinn parked on its kickstand in the living room. Instead, like an enormous gold and brown butterfly agleam in the early sunlight, a Steinway grand piano stood in the living room alcove, its strings and pale blond sound board reflected in its open lid. Dad caught my eye and shook his head. Mom was talking to the deliverymen. Her back was turned, so she didn't see Dad put his finger to his lips. He came closer, put his arm around my shoulder. "Be patient, Dana," he whispered. "Christmas is just around the corner." I brushed away my tears and tried to smile.

"This was Mama's piano, Dana," Mom told me. "Grandpa wanted you to have a real piano, so he sent it to New York City, to the Steinway company, to have it rebuilt for you."

Tom and Ben crawled under the Steinway, laughing. "Can we make a fort?"

Mom shushed them. "Would you play something for us, Dana?"

I was just tall enough to sit on the piano bench without help. I played Mozart's minuet in G major, which I'd memorized. Each note, each chord seemed to rise and hover in the room, lingering there, like an echo. Just as I finished, I heard the dolly roll across the driveway, watched the deliverymen lift and load my upright piano into the panel truck.

o o o

I found the score of Beethoven's "Für Elise" in one of my grandmother's boxes, stored in the attic, and learned it on my own to surprise Mrs. Parker, my piano teacher. After I played it for her the first time, she went over it with me measure by measure, noting my grandmother's fingering and pedal marks, pointing out the diminuendos and crescendos and repeats. We both laughed at the exclamation points my grandmother had penciled in, reminders to pay attention. Thanks to Mrs. Parker, my grandmother, and Beethoven, I discovered that learning to play a piece of music involved more than getting the notes right. Much more. Thanks to my grandmother's piano, I learned the joy of playing each note, hearing depth and breadth, textures that I could create and control.

Five years later, a month after my thirteenth birthday, Mrs. Parker moved to California with her daughter and her family. At our last lesson, she gave me a plastic bust of Beethoven. There was a small bookcase next to the piano in the alcove. I sat Beethoven on the shelf next to the photograph of my grandmother. In it, dressed in a long-sleeved, floor-length gown—dark blue velvet, my mother had told me—a white orchid pinned to the shoulder of her right sleeve, she sat at her Steinway, hands on the keyboard, her hair in a braid coiled around her head.

"Beethoven and your grandmother. From now on, you'll be playing for them both," Mrs. Parker told me.

After school, I sometimes placed Beethoven's bust and the photograph on the music desk next to my music. I'd play a scale, then stop and look at them, imagining their comments. Speaking in a low, gruff rumble (in English, of course), Beethoven would urge me to slow down. My grandmother, her voice just like my mother's, would tell me it sounded "just wonderful." Then she'd suggest I play the scale again, three octaves this time, in triplets, starting pianissimo, building to fortissimo, then diminuendo back to pianissimo. Beethoven liked it that way too.

o o o

After Mrs. Parker left, I had to find another teacher. At the end of the summer, right before school started, my mother announced that she had scheduled an audition for me with Mademoiselle Arnaut. People said she had studied with Debussy at the Paris Conservatory. She only accepted serious students—the promising ones, the ones who appeared to have Juilliard or Curtis stamped on their foreheads. Even kids who didn't take piano lessons knew about her.

"Your audition is next Monday."

That gave me four days to prepare. "I'm *really* not good enough, Mom."

"How do you know?"

"Because Jimmy's one of her students." Talented and conceited, Jimmy Bauer was my age and had had a crush on me since fourth grade. He'd begun lessons at three and practiced five hours a day. At last year's talent show, he had played Chopin's "Revolutionary Étude". Kids had cheered. My mother wanted me to become a "serious student" like Jimmy. She was sure Mademoiselle Arnaut would show me the way.

"I told her how long you'd studied, that you just turned thirteen, that you practice every day. She seems to think you're advanced enough."

"What does she want me to play?"

"Whatever you like."

After hearing it on the radio, I'd learned to play Grieg's "Butterfly" on my own. It had been my going-away gift to Mrs. Parker. I knew it by heart and enjoyed playing it. What did I have to lose, after all? Maybe the spirits of Grieg, my grandmother, and Mrs. Parker would carry me through the audition. Anyway, it didn't matter to me if Mademoiselle Arnaut didn't accept me.

"I'll play the Grieg, then."

The more I practiced over the next few days, the more my fingers skidded and slipped. Sections I'd played flawlessly just the week before fell apart. At the time, I didn't realize I had a bad case of stage fright. Hadn't I said I didn't care how the audition turned out?

I barely slept Sunday night, playing the piece over and over in my head. Just before I got up, prepared to tell my mother I would rather die than play for Mademoiselle Arnaut, Jimmy Bauer's taunting smile came into view, provoking an adrenaline rush that quieted the butterflies: I would succeed with Mademoiselle, if only to prove to Jimmy that I could.

On Monday afternoon, during the four-mile drive from Middletown to Newport before my audition, Mom and I didn't speak.

Glancing at me from time to time, she gripped the wheel with both hands. I realized then that she was apprehensive, too. I looked out the window at the breakers pounding Easton's Beach, at the seagulls wheeling above the surf, at a boat—fishing boat or lobsterman—on the horizon.

"Jimmy will find out I auditioned even if Mademoiselle doesn't accept me."

"Let's just get through the audition, shall we?"

"We, white man?" This was one of Ben's favorite lines. Mom laughed.

"Pretend you're playing for Mrs Parker. And Beethoven." This time, we both laughed.

o o o

Mademoiselle's apartment and piano studio were on the second floor of a three-story Victorian house near Newport harbor. Converted into apartments in the 1920s, the house towered over the two-story eighteenth-century clapboard cottages that lined the streets around it.

Mom rang the bell. When a buzzer sounded, we opened the door to the entryway and gazed at the painting on the walls and ceiling. A trompe-l'oeil trumpet vine, festooned with buds, blooms, butterflies, and hummingbirds, wound its way from the first floor all the way to the third. When Mom noticed the butterflies, she nodded at them, and smiled at me.

Standing at the banister of the second-floor landing, Mademoiselle waved us up the stairs. Five feet tall, birdlike, her hair dyed reddish-brown, she wore a pale pink sweater, a calf-length tweed skirt, and a silk scarf loosely knotted around her neck and draped over her shoulders. Her eyebrows plucked, she had penciled them in, and her eyes were heavily outlined in black. (Mom explained later that this had been the French fashion when Mademoiselle was in her twenties. When I pointed out that Mademoiselle was probably in her late eighties now, Mom laughed. "She's French, Dana, so she knows from style. Those eyebrows are her signature, just like her silk Hermès scarf.")

On the landing, to the left of the studio door, sat two small armchairs and a table with stacks of *Paris Match*, *l'Express*, and French *Vogue*. Through the open door, I could see the tail of Mademoiselle's piano, its lid open to the room beyond.

Mademoiselle shook my mother's hand, then gestured at the chairs and the magazines. "Please, Madame. You will wait for us here."

"First, listen. Then, talk," she said as she ushered me into the studio.

Mom blew me an air kiss. I didn't give her a chance to hug me.

In the studio, shelves of books and music scores lined two of the walls. Framed botanical prints and paintings—Paris street scenes and a few landscapes—hung above the sofa against the wall to the left of the door. Across the room from the piano, a bay window with a window seat looked out through the branches of a large maple to Newport harbor a block away.

Mademoiselle took my jacket and laid it on the sofa. She nodded at her piano, a medium grand. "My Steinway was built in 1936." She patted it and smiled. "One of the best."

I thought about my own Steinway (built in 1919, I wanted to tell her), and my grandmother, and Beethoven, waiting for me at home.

Mademoiselle closed the piano lid, pulled out a straight-backed chair, and set it down to the right of the piano bench—close enough to watch my hands without getting in my way. "You may begin."

She didn't ask what I would play for her. That surprised me. And, somehow, set me free. No longer nervous, I anticipated playing a piece I loved, a piece I enjoyed for its delicate evocation of butterflies in flight. If I didn't play it well enough to meet her standards, so be it.

She sat motionless, holding a small notebook and fountain pen, as I adjusted the height of the bench and ran my hands lightly over the keys, the ivory brighter—because newer? —than mine. Without asking, without hesitating, I played a B-flat scale, a G-major scale, then several arpeggios to warm up. Light and lively, the piano's action felt familiar, its tone, even in the upper register, warm and clear.

A bird called. Outside the window, a cardinal perched on a branch, head turned toward me. I began.

Mademoiselle shifted in her chair, leaning forward, listening.

I played the piece without a single slip. Its dreaminess and lightness wafted through the room like a gentle air current. When I finished, I waited for Mademoiselle. Except for the sound of her pen, as she made notes, the room was silent. How many others had sat like this, waiting for her to pass judgment?

When she looked up at me, there was something in her expression, something in her eyes—narrowed, calculating—eyes that told me I'd surprised—even impressed—her. "That's a lovely piece," she said. "I've played it often. Once for a recital when I was a student at the *Conservatoire*." She smiled. "Many people assume these pieces—the ones in the collection, I mean—are *faciles*, 'easy', for beginners. But, you know, they are not at all 'easy' pieces." She shook her head. Her mocking laugh passed judgement on the "many" who were, in her view, wrongheaded.

"Who are your favorite composers?" she asked.

"Bach. Beethoven. And Schubert. And Chopin." My voice sounded older, confident and relaxed. "And Ravel."

She didn't ask what pieces I knew by heart, or which ones I had played and why I liked them. This wasn't a conversation. She was evaluating my attitude and how much I knew. Was I serious enough to merit her time and attention?

"Do you like to sightread?" Under the penciled arches of her eyebrows, her brown eyes focused on mine, bright and birdlike.

"I don't know."

"You don't know how?"

"Do you have to learn how?"

"Oh my, yes." She made a note.

Often, when I finished practicing, I opened one of my grand-mother's scores—Bach's partitas, Mozart's sonatas—and selected something new, doing my best to ignore the notes I missed, to hear the music I knew was there, hidden for now from view. Usually, I gave up. Too many wrong notes.

"Once you've had more experience, you'll see. Sightreading is like meeting someone for the first time, someone you want to know better. Take it slow at first." She smiled. "You will enjoy playing more."

I wanted to tell her about Jeanne-Marie Darré's performance of Chopin's Ballade in g minor at Carnegie Hall, about the notes rising like schools of tropical fish to where I sat in the balcony, about buying the score for the Ballade, trying to learn it, wanting to play like Mme Darré, but she closed her notebook and placed the cap on her pen.

"*C'est bien, alors.*" She smoothed her skirt, gave her scarf a little tug, and gestured at the sofa. She crossed the room and opened the door. "Please, Madame. You may come in now."

Mom smiled and sat down beside me on the sofa. Seated in the armchair facing us, Mademoiselle crossed her ankles and reached behind her to adjust the cushion. "She plays quite well, your daughter," she said, glancing down at her notebook. "She is musical, and she has talent. If she works hard, she could be quite good."

Mom nodded and patted my hand.

Sometimes, alone at home, practicing, I fantasized about playing in Carnegie Hall, imagining the applause and the calls for an encore. I practiced my bow and my smile in front of the full-length mirror in the upstairs hallway. Of course, I knew it would take more than bows and smiles to be a concert artist. The nausea that overcame me at the very thought of performing in public, anywhere, let alone Carnegie Hall, left my hands wet, clammy, and inert. Would I ever be "quite good" enough to give a concert?

As we said goodbye, Mademoiselle Arnaut promised we would hear from her soon.

On the way home, I cried. "'Quite good'? It's like I said, Mom. I'm not good enough."

Mom fished out a tissue for me.

"Be patient, Dana. She'll send a letter, she said. Someone like Mademoiselle—"

"You mean, someone whose students all play like Jimmy?"

She pushed on. "To Mademoiselle, 'quite good' may be the next-to-last stop on the way to 'very good.' Look, Dana, if you were already 'very good,' you'd be enrolled in the NEC Preparatory Program, and we'd be living in Boston."

"What if she doesn't accept me?"

"I'll keep looking."

Mom had her heart set on Mademoiselle Arnaut. I couldn't tell her that anyone but Mademoiselle would be fine with me.

o o o

The acceptance letter arrived the following week. I read and reread Mademoiselle's comments, trying to figure out why what she said didn't make me feel better about my playing. What was missing? I was "promising," "a hard worker," "musical," she wrote. She didn't say she could tell I was "serious." Although she had told Mom I was "talented," she didn't say that in her letter. Even I knew that talent was what set "serious" apart from "good enough."

"She could tell from the way you played that you practice, that you work hard," Mom said. "Give yourself a chance."

I didn't dare tell Mom what I knew. Or that I had hoped Mademoiselle wouldn't accept me. That afternoon, I sat at the piano, holding my grandmother's photograph, trying to imagine what she was thinking, trying to imagine what she would advise me to do. She had been a talented pianist, a professional. That much I knew. But she had stopped playing the piano. I didn't know why. Did she, too, suffer from the fear of not being good enough?

At a lesson one time, before Mrs. Parker moved away, struggling with one of the fugues from Bach's Well-Tempered Clavichord, I kept making the same mistake. Finally, I slammed the keyboard cover closed and jumped up. "I hate the piano! I hate Bach!"

Mrs. Parker held my hands while I cried. When I calmed down, she talked to me about her dreams of becoming a concert pianist. "I wanted that more than anything. I practiced so hard. But, like you, I had difficulties—technical problems for one, and memorizing for another. Every time I played in public, I had memory blanks."

In the end, she realized she would never be good enough to be a star. "I didn't have the talent. And besides, I wanted other things in life, like marriage, and children. As a concert artist I'd have spent most of my life travelling, concertizing." She smiled. "I knew if I did that, playing the piano, which I loved to do, would soon become drudgery. But I continued and eventually became quite good at it. I enjoy playing. And I enjoy teaching. That's good enough for me. Don't give up, Dana. You'll see. You'll find your way."

I decided to go ahead with Mademoiselle. It didn't matter what I chose to do in the future. Not yet.

o o o

At first, my lessons with Mademoiselle felt like walking on thin ice. She never smiled, never encouraged me. Sometimes she would stop me as soon as I began and have me play the same phrase over and over throughout the hour. No matter how hard I tried, it seemed I couldn't satisfy her. But I didn't want to disappoint Mom, even though there were times I wished for a broken bone, or a fatal illness—anything to avoid my lesson.

A year later, one rainy March afternoon, I arrived a few minutes late for my lesson. I began to play the Schubert Impromptu I was learning for the annual recital. Halfway through, I realized Mademoiselle was listening, eyes closed, leaning back in her chair. Usually she sat up straight, scrutinizing me. As soon as I played the last chord, she leaned forward

"*C'est très bien*, Dana. Very good." Quickly she went over the score, pointing out places that still needed work. None of her comments got through. All I could hear was, "*C'est très bien*, Dana."

"I played "Clair de Lune" for Debussy himself when I was sixteen, you know. He told me he couldn't have played it better." She looked down at her hands. "That was my proudest day," she said, a faraway look in her eyes. She had been a rising star until she shattered her left wrist in a bicycle accident.

Mom hugged me when I told her. "See? That's what she saw when you auditioned. You can do this."

Mom was right about one thing, at least. For months, I'd been learning how to practice. And becoming good at doing what I was told. "You must pay attention all the time," Mademoiselle admonished me. "If you don't correct your mistakes right away, they will follow you wherever you go, whenever you play—for me, or anyone else. Slow practice, hands separate, first. Then slow practice, hands together. You're training your muscles, yes. You're also training your brain. If you do this right, they won't let you down." Her eyes narrowed. "You must listen to yourself, Dana. Mistakes only happen when you're inattentive." Did she realize she was rubbing her left wrist?

Mademoiselle's system worked for me once I began to play more complex pieces. Analyzing and practicing phrases, linking them, helped me to develop my technique—and to memorize. With each new piece I learned, I became more confident.

But the more confident I became, the less I enjoyed playing. I didn't begin to understand why until two years later, after the competition.

o o o

My junior year, the application for the annual city-wide piano competition arrived in February. After work, before she made dinner, Mom came into the living room with a cup of tea. Distracted, I fumbled.

"How's it going today?"

I was working on Debussy's "Clair de Lune." It terrified me. I couldn't help thinking about Mademoiselle playing it for Debussy himself.

"Not so great. I screw up something different each time I play it through." It takes time to build muscle memory, time to hear the piece in your own head, to know its structure so well it's as if you had composed it yourself. So far—with this piece, anyway—all of this was still a work in progress.

I ran my fingers over the keys, cool and inert. Sometimes they felt smooth and fluid, like flowing water. At others, they felt like ice floes separated by uneven gaps, crashing together as they raced down a turbulent river.

Mom cleared her throat. "Mademoiselle thinks it would be good for you to enter the competition this year," she said. "You'll start preparing now; then you'll have the summer." Her eyes brushed over me, checking my reaction. "You'll have time for your schoolwork, of course. But nothing extra."

I had been playing the piano for eight years, but the idea of playing for strangers was about as appealing as having my fingernails pulled out. When I played for myself, for Mom, or for Mademoiselle, my butterflies perched, quiescent in the shadows. So far, I hadn't been able to admit to my fear of playing in public—not to Mom, and certainly not to Mademoiselle.

"What about my job?" I liked my part-time summer job at the library—two, sometimes three, hours shelving books every afternoon. It wasn't as boring as it sounds, because I got to walk to and from the library, along the beach, and check out new books. Usually, I took my Walkman and listened to recordings of pieces I was learning. Mademoiselle wouldn't have approved. But she didn't know. What I knew is that it helped me hear new pieces without having to think about them. Someone else was in charge. I could relax and enjoy the music.

"We'll have to see if you have time for that."

I decided not to push my luck. "Wait and see" might work this time.

"What about Jimmy?"

"What do you mean?"

"Will he be competing?"

"Of course."

After my first month of lessons with Mademoiselle, Jimmy had cornered me in the cafeteria. "How's it going, Dana?"

"Fine."

"With Mademoiselle, I mean."

"That's what I meant, too."

"She's pretty easy, at least at the beginning."

"Really?" Ignoring his smirk, I walked away.

Thanks to Mademoiselle, I learned to enjoy practicing. Everything that was new and out of control in the beginning eventually settled into a state of comfort and familiarity once I'd mastered her method. The steps to connecting the notes on the page to my fingers on the keys resembled dissection. Having dissected a frog, I knew about muscles, tendons, and joints, how they worked. So, the mechanics of piano practice weren't a mystery. But there was more to making music than physical coordination.

As soon as summer vacation began, I got up and practiced for two hours every morning, working my way through each of the three selections for the competition, getting the notes in my fingers. This was a mostly mechanical exercise. At this early stage, I was playing the notes. And the music? Was it too much to hope that would come later?

Then I met Jean.

◦ ◦ ◦

On my way home from the library every afternoon, I passed Joe's Café. Weathered siding, wraparound deck, and college-age waitstaff—it was one among several bars and restaurants opposite the beach on East Main Road. It was the only place that featured live music daily from midafternoon until midnight. The owner, Joe, a retired jazz bassist, had connections. And an interest in promoting young musicians.

One afternoon, a virtuoso accordionist was playing an unfamiliar tune—a fast two-step. I climbed the steps to the deck and peered in. A quartet (fiddle, guitar, drums, washboard) accompanied the accordionist. His voice soared and swooped, singing a song in a language I didn't recognize. The guy playing the washboard ran a spoon up, down, and around it, producing a rhythmic, raucous clatter. This was called a "frottoir," I learned later, an instrument traditional to zydeco.

Dressed in a muscle shirt and jeans, the singer hopped and stamped around the stage, his shoulder-length dreads bobbing, arms pumping the accordion, fingers racing up and down its keyboard. His glossy baritone blended with the fiddle tune, weaving around and through the accordion's accompaniment.

By the time the band took a break, a small crowd had joined me on the deck, clapping and dancing. Wiping his face with a towel, the singer caught my eye. He put the accordion down on a stand and spoke over his shoulder to the others.

On the steps, as the crowd broke up, he introduced himself. "Name's Jean, but you can call me *Jean*," he said. "And you are?"

"Dana, Dana Carlson," I said. He was looking into the sun. Could he see I was blushing?

"Can I buy you a drink, Dana?"

"Iced tea?" My voice cracked. He didn't seem to notice.

"I can handle that." He had a hint of an accent, maybe French, but not like Mademoiselle's. His accent was warm and soft, more like a drawl; hers was prickly, like the wind in your face.

He went back inside. The phrase *da capo al fine*, "take it from the top," was tattooed across his shoulders, just above his sleeveless T-shirt. In classical music, this phrase cues the musician to repeat a section from the beginning (*capo*) to the end (*fine*). So, this guy, an ace accordionist, was also a classical musician?

He handed me my iced tea and sat down on the steps with a cup of coffee. "You from around here?" His tone of voice, his half-smile, told me he knew the answer.

"I live up there," I told him, pointing in the direction of my neighborhood above the beach. "What about you?"

"Dad's from Haiti. Mom's from Martinique. I was born in New Orleans. I'm in school now in Boston. I'm a junior—NEC, the conservatory?"

So I was right about the classical music part. "This is just a summer job?"

"The drummer knows Joe from his other restaurant. He's in one of my classes. He got the gig. The accordion player he signed up had to go home for the summer. So, here I am. At your service, mamzelle." He pretended to doff a hat and grinned.

I wondered how Mademoiselle would react if I called her "mamzelle."

"You like zydeco?" He asked as if he knew the answer but wanted to hear it anyway.

"Zydeco?" My tongue prickled, as though I'd eaten something peppery.

"What we've been playing." He sipped and savored his coffee for a moment before swallowing. "It's Louisiana Creole music."

"What's 'creole,'" I asked.

"It's a kind of French. My family's kind. Zydeco? Long story; a lot of history." He gave his dreads a shake and smiled. "I'll tell you about it sometime." I smiled at his certainty there would be another time.

He stood and tossed his empty cup into the trashcan.

I looked around. A few people, summer people, sat on the hoods and bumpers of cars, waiting for the break to end.

"I've got half an hour. Can I give you a lift?"

"Now?" My head spun as if there'd been something stronger than lemon juice in my iced tea.

"No time like the present." He laughed.

So did I.

Jean waved at a blue Suzuki parked under a tree. "Your ride, mamzelle." He removed two helmets from the storage compartment behind the seat. "Room enough for two."

I put on the helmet and got behind him. Everything slowed down. Zydeco. Louisiana Creole. Jean and his motorcycle. Up close, his skin gleamed; the tattoo across his shoulders rippled when he moved his arms. I would have asked him to take the long way home, but there wasn't one.

"S'okay to put your arms around me," Jean said. "Or you can hang on to my belt." He laughed, gunned the motor, and headed out of the parking lot, away from town and Joe's. The drummer tipped his hat as we rode by.

The fragrance of wild roses and the brackish scent of Easton's Pond followed us along the beach, past sunbathers and volleyball players. Too soon, Jean downshifted and turned up our driveway. Mom, at the kitchen sink, looked out, then disappeared.

She met us outside the gate. Jean parked the bike, removed his helmet, and shook out his dreads. Mom didn't move. Or smile.

"This is Jean, Mom."

Jean smiled at her and held out his hand. "Jean Lemaitre."

As she shook his hand, Mom sized him up: skin color, muscle shirt, dreads, and the Suzuki. *Wait 'til she sees the tattoo.*

"Hello." My mother stared past him across the road.

"Very pleased to meet you," Jean said.

"Would you like to come in, Jean?" I started toward the house.

Mom stepped toward me, between us. "I left some green beans in the colander, Dana. Would you wash them? And set the table? I'm going to pick up Dad."

Jean put on his helmet. His back to my mom, he winked at me and smiled. "Bye now, Dana." He let the bike coast down the driveway, turning the engine on when he reached the road.

"A tattoo? Really, Dana?"

There was no point trying to explain then what I knew about Jean, what the tattoo meant about him. I'd have my chance later when Dad came home.

o o o

A half-hour later, my parents came into the kitchen. Mom dropped her keys on the counter and crossed her arms. "A stranger on a motorcycle?"

"He's a musician, Mom. He's got a summer job at Joe's."

She glanced at Dad.

"He brought me home, didn't he?"

Dad poured a drink. Mom shook her head. "He's too old for you. And he's not from around here."

Jean would have to be nineteen to play at Joe's Café. Maybe he was twenty since he was a junior at NEC. Still, I knew better than to argue the point.

Dad loosened his tie and sipped his drink. Mom didn't bring up the dreads. Or that Jean was Black. I could tell she already had.

"You signed the contract, honey. No dates in cars until you're seventeen." Dad thought contracts were the solution to every problem. You read the terms; you agreed to the terms; you signed on the bottom line, accepting the penalty for non-compliance.

"A ride home isn't a date."

"Really," she said. "For the rest of the month, I'll pick you up from the library." She looked at Dad. Her look said, "I told you so." Dad drained his glass.

o o o

I knew Mom bragged that she never had to worry about me—unlike Tom, who never met a rule he didn't challenge. I learned early that doing as I was told made my mother happy. I'd never crossed the line before.

Later, lying in bed in the dark, I thought about *da capo al fine* and about going back to the beginning, starting over, with changes along the way—changes I would choose for myself. I couldn't relive the last sixteen years. But I could start paying attention to what was going on behind the scenes, who I was becoming, and learn how to make changes that mattered to me, first.

In the morning, I read Mom's note: "I'll be there at 4:30. Wait for me." I crumpled it up, tossed it in the trash, and spent the morning practicing. The selection of pieces for the competition included a prelude and fugue from Bach's Well-Tempered Clavichord, a Schubert Impromptu, and Debussy's "La plus que lente." Until the day of the competition, I wouldn't know which piece I would play for the judges. They would draw their selection from a hat.

At noon, I walked into town, to the library, wondering if I'd see Jean again. I cringed, remembering Mom's look, a look he couldn't have missed. Jean and the band weren't at Joe's yet, so I didn't stop.

Two blocks from the library, I heard the motorcycle behind me.

Jean pulled up next to me, stopped, and got off. "Was it bad?"

I shrugged. I couldn't look him in the eye.

He smiled. "First time?"

I nodded.

"The bike?"

"Yeah. Plus, they think you're too old for me." I couldn't tell him that his being Black was an issue, too. I wondered if I hadn't accept-ed the ride, if I had brought Jean home and introduced him like any other boy they didn't know, Mom and Dad would have been more accepting.

"How old are you?"

"Sixteen."

He let out a long, low whistle and smiled. "S'okay. We'll deal." Pushing the bike along, he walked me to the corner, just out of sight of the library's front door.

"No use advertising it, right?" He nodded toward the library, touched his finger to his lips, and ran it along my cheek. "Later." Half-way up the block, he slowed, stopped, and called back to me, "Nine-teen!"

o o o

At dinner, Dad did his best to distract us. "Remember Mrs. DeWitt?"

Mom puffed out her cheeks and sighed.

"Her neighbor is trying to sue her. Again." Loud laugh. Too loud. "Same reason, of course. She leaves her dog tied up outside all day and it barks nonstop." Big sigh. Shrug. "So, here's what the judge did. He told Mrs. DeWitt he'd have her dog repossessed if she didn't keep it indoors."

Mom sipped her wine. I kept my head down.

"Don't you get it?" He glanced at Mom, then at me, as if we didn't already know how hard he was trying. "You can't have a dog repos-sessed. It's not like a car. But the threat did the trick. He's something else, that judge." He sighed and got up.

Mom pushed her chair back.

I cleared the table and loaded the dishwasher.

o o o

After I'd gone to bed, they sat on the patio under my window talking about Lil, who had run away with Marco—on a motorcycle—when she was seventeen. Marco was twenty-three. Even the FBI got involved in the search.

"I had to go home for a week the month before I graduated from college to help find her. Never again, Matt."

"Dana's not Lil, Grace." Dad's tone, soothing, placating, drifted up to me.

My cheek still tingled where Jean had touched it. In the moonlit sky above the trees outside my bedroom window, he floated, whispering, "No worries. We'll deal."

o o o

The next morning, I opened the French doors to the patio. The garden and trees glistened after a night of fog. Even the piano keys were slick. I dried them one by one. Mom and Dad had left early to spend the day in Boston with friends.

The mockingbird in our magnolia tree trilled and whistled. Alone in the quiet house, I warmed up with scales and arpeggios, then began to play the Debussy waltz "La plus que lente."

With Mademoiselle, before I began to learn a piece, I studied the score, which she had marked up: fingering (in pencil) the dynamics (red for *forte*, blue for *piano*), learning where phrases began and ended, identifying fingering challenges and tempo changes, listening to it in my head. Some pianists listen to recordings of different interpretations as they begin to work on a piece. Mademoiselle frowned on this. The interpretation she knew, the one she passed on to me in her markings on the score, was always her own. Except for "La plus que lente." She assured me her interpretation was Debussy's.

"You must hear the music in your own head, Dana," she told me. She pronounced my name "DahNah." "If you listen to recordings, you'll just imitate what you hear. And if you have a memory lapse? What happens then? If you haven't been listening to yourself from the very first time you played the piece, you'll be lost."

I understood what she meant. Too often, what came out of the piano wasn't at all what I heard in my head. Today was one of those times. So I stopped. I couldn't fix what was wrong by repeating the same passage over and over.

I had just closed the score when Jean cleared his throat. He stood on the patio, helmet in hand.

I waved him in.

He put his shoes next to his helmet on the mat by the door and came over to the piano. "May I?" He leaned over the soundboard, as if listening to its secrets. Of course, I told him about my grandmother and showed him the photograph. "Before he died, my grandfather had the piano restored for me. For my eighth birthday."

He let out a low whistle, "That's some birthday present."

"I wanted a bicycle."

"And you got a Rolls Royce instead," Jean grinned.

While I was telling Jean the story, he wandered around the room, pausing at the shelves of trophies on the near side of the fireplace.

"Your brother's?"

"Tom's, yes. He's the older one."

"And the younger one?"

"Ben is an artist." I had never said this before. None of us had. For the first time, I realized it was true. This was Ben's truth. "He did those pen-and-ink drawings."

In the drawings of different flowering plants—a daffodil, a sunflower, a Japanese iris—the details of every leaf, stem, and petal gave each plant such depth and texture, each one appeared three-dimensional. Mom had once called Ben's drawings plant portraits. Seeing them now through Jean's eyes, I understood what she meant.

Jean took a closer look. "You can feel the leaves, smell the fragrance, almost, can't you?" He turned and gestured at the piano. "I've got an idea about that passage you're working on. May I?"

It was as if he'd read my mind. Mademoiselle had left for France a month ago. Although she'd prepared a detailed practice plan for me, it didn't answer my questions. The plan couldn't listen to me and comment. Especially, I needed the reassurance I heard in Jean's voice—reassurance that I didn't have to do this on my own.

"Please."

He sat to my left on the bench, close but not touching.

"Hold my arm, right there." He positioned my left hand just under his right elbow and began to play the passage without looking at the score. The weight of his wrist and forearm lay loose and free in my hand as he played the first phrase.

"See? When you settle into the keyboard, you get this open, full sound." He turned, straddling the bench, motioning to me to do the same. Holding my right wrist in his left hand to steady my arm, he positioned his right hand on my forearm, lifting and dropping each finger, one at a time, his wrist relaxed. My skin tingled.

"Your turn." He swiveled back around and inched over to his left to give me more room.

I started to play, relaxing, linking the weight of my arm through my wrist and hands to the keyboard. I could feel the difference; hear it, too. The tension in my neck released. Now the waltz melody seemed to swing over the accompaniment. And my touch was secure in the keys from the moment I began. I took my time going into the downbeats—even my breathing slowed—as I finished the phrase.

"You're pretty good at this, you know?"

Mademoiselle's comment that I played "quite well" still resonated, a reminder that being "musical" wasn't enough. If I was "pretty good" in Jean's eyes, though, that was good enough for me.

"What do you see when you're playing this piece?"

"What do you mean?"

"Let me play it for you. Close your eyes. Let your mind drift. Remember that Debussy called this a slow waltz—actually, a slower than slow waltz. He wanted you to understand that we're not in Vienna, that this isn't a Strauss waltz. It's more of an impression of a waltz. Like a dream or a memory. It's up to you, the pianist, to recreate that impression so that the listener, too, can feel it."

I sat on the sofa, eyes closed, listening, imagining dancers moving across a stage or a dance floor: the men in waistcoats, the women in ball gowns, swaying as they circled the floor, their shadows floating like petals on the surface of a pond, brushed gently by the breeze.

When Jean finished, I played the piece again, feeling the breeze, the languid pulse of the dancers circling the floor.

"That's what I mean," Jean said. "That's lovely."

"Duets?" He pointed at the cabinet where I kept my music.

"Take your pick."

We played Schubert, Mozart, and Brahms. By now, I could sightread well enough to enjoy the challenge. Jean hummed along or whispered encouragement. Every time my forearm brushed his or our feet happened to collide over the pedal, we adjusted. "It's like dancing, trying to remember—to feel—who's leading," I said.

Jean laughed. "That's one of the reasons I want to conduct."

"So you can lead all the time?"

He grinned.

Our music teacher at school conducted the school orchestra. We needed him to keep time, but there wasn't much else he did for us. Of course, what Jean was talking about was different.

At 1:00 o'clock, he stood and stretched. "Gotta go," he said. "You too, right?"

As we walked toward town he told me about his classes—at Berklee and at NEC—and the gig at Joe's. He'd taken it for the summer to pay for Berklee so his parents wouldn't know he'd enrolled in jazz classes there. "My father. He tried that life. Then, he met my mom. For her, it was a package deal. If he wanted to marry her, he had to find real work. Now he's an accountant. But he still plays, a little. Classical, now, that's a whole other story. That's what they want for me."

"So, conduct Beethoven, play zydeco on the side?"

He grinned. "That's the idea, anyway."

We stopped at the intersection near Joe's. Steam rising from the wet pavement swirled around us. As the fog lifted, the sound of the surf grew louder.

"Come to Joe's tonight?"

"My parents. Well, you know…." I looked at him.

He smiled and brushed a strand of hair off my forehead. "I'll pick you up at your place and we can walk down together. It's only a couple miles. You'll be home before midnight. They'll never know."

o o o

When Dad called at six, I told him I'd practiced and gone to work as usual, a half-truth that made my heart pound.

"We'll be home after midnight," he said.

"I'll be in bed by then." If all went as Jean and I had planned, this part, anyway, would be true.

I hung up. Out of breath, as if I'd been running, I drank a glass of water, gasping as it spilled down the front of my T-shirt.

The piano lid was still open. I sat down and played Chopin's Revolutionary Etude, the piece I had played at my last recital. Its runs rose and fell like waves cresting, then tumbling on the beach. I laughed. Some revolution.

Jean knocked on the back door at nine. The porch light glowed in the mist. We felt our way down the driveway and along the dirt shoulder of the road into town. Occasionally, he reached out and touched my arm, his fingers warm and dry. When we came to the streetlight at the intersection, he took my hand.

Joe's was packed. Mostly tourists, as far as I could tell. Except the group in the corner, sitting at a table behind the bar—Jean's band and their girlfriends, their eyes on us, as we crossed the floor. Like the other girls, I wore jeans and a sleeveless tank top. Unlike them, I was underage. They pulled a chair over for me.

As the band warmed up for their first set, I went to the far corner of the dance floor. I wanted to listen and dance, not talk. They started with the same two-step they'd been playing when I'd first heard them. The next number, a slow waltz, was a zydeco version of "La plus que lente." I waved and clapped when the fiddle eased into a bluesy rendition of the melody. When Jean played it on the accordion, the chords in the bass breathed into the downbeats. More than a variation, the band's version was an original, the way jazz renditions of familiar tunes always are. I knew then I'd never again hear—or play— the piece without thinking of this one, this night.

Listening to this adaptation of "La plus que lente," I thought about Jean's tattoo, *da capo al fine*, which I now saw in a new light. Whether you play it, or someone else does, every performance of a piece you know well differs from all others. Exciting—and terrifying when you're the performer. Anything can happen. I could learn the notes and develop my technique. But how could I prepare for the unexpected? How could I make *da capo al fine* work for me?

During the first break, Jean and I went out to the parking lot. When he pulled me to him, what began as a hug turned into a kiss that lasted until I stepped back to take a breath.

Jean slid his fingers up the back of my neck into my hair, giving me a little shake. "Again?"

This time, I breathed with him.

o o o

At eleven thirty, the beginning of the next break, Jean waved me over to the back door. Arm around my shoulders, he guided me along the road toward home. We could hear the waves crashing, feel the thud of the surf on the beach under our feet. Thicker now, the fog transformed the streetlights, the neon signs, and the traffic lights into glowing smudges of gold, green, and red.

"What do you want to do with the piano?" he asked me.

"Just get through the competition, for now."

"Hard work." The smile in his voice carried through the fog.

"The Bach, Schubert, and Debussy, from breakfast to noon. And sometimes after work."

"Which Schubert?"

"Opus 142, no. 3."

He let out a long, low whistle. "One of my favorites."

"Mine too, now. But I don't get it."

"What's not to get?"

"The whole program. I'm learning the notes. But am I learning the music?"

Each piece held its own perils. "It seems like no matter how much I practice, every time I play a piece, it's the first time all over again." I had to ask. "Is that how it is for you?"

"Always. But that's good. It keeps the music fresh, which counts in performance. What about your teacher? What does she think?"

"I haven't asked. She's away for the summer." I didn't tell him that Mademoiselle encouraged me to play the pieces the same way, each time. I couldn't tell him I could only ask her questions about practical details, not interpretation.

We had reached the foot of the driveway, drenched and shivering. "I'll wait here 'til you're in the house." He caressed my cheek. "You start practicing at nine?"

"My parents leave at eight thirty every morning."

"'Til tomorrow, then. Nine-thirty sharp."

At the front door, I turned to look for him. He had disappeared. A car came down the hill, fog swirling around its high beams as it slowed and headed up our driveway.

I kicked off my sandals and ran back through the patio around the house to the back door. Behind me, the car doors slammed. I could hear my parents' voices, and laughter, as they came up the front walk. I took the stairs two at a time in the dark, tiptoed down the hallway to my room, and huddled under the covers, out of breath, listening to my pounding heart.

o o o

Thorough as it was, Mademoiselle's practice plan lacked one essential ingredient: there was no one who could listen to me and give me pointers while she was away. Sure, I played for my parents, but to them almost anything sounded "just fine, dear." So, when Jean offered to coach me, I didn't hesitate.

By unspoken agreement, we didn't discuss what (or if) I would tell my parents about our arrangement. If we timed Jean's arrivals and departures right, they'd never know. Most mornings, he arrived at nine-thirty, settled on the sofa with a cup of coffee, and spread the scores open on the coffee table. By then I'd had enough time to warm up and review what we'd worked on the day before. Every day, I varied the order, starting with the last piece I'd played the previous day and working backwards through the program. This had been Jean's idea: "You won't be in the habit of starting the same way. When you get to the competition, you'll be comfortable playing the piece they choose."

Jean's suggestions for changes in tempo and phrasing helped bring each piece into focus. Mademoiselle had framed everything in terms of precision and clarity—crescendo to here, release pedal there. As if standing on a mountaintop, surveying cloud shadows passing over the fields below, Jean talked to me about how each phrase connected to the next, how the voicing could be adjusted in the repeats to bring out new features. This is how I learned the value of *da capo al fine* as a concept, and how I began to tame my fear of the unexpected.

"What isn't written down—ever—is that you're supposed to repeat the passage but not play it the same way. Sounds self-evident, right? We're not machines. The music lives and breathes through us. But it's deeper than that. You can make small changes in dynamics and emphasis. So, the 'da capo' gives you a fresh start. Think of it like this," he said. "You're creating a soundscape, painting a picture in sound. Close your eyes for a minute. Listen." He played the Bach prelude through. "What do you see?"

I took my time. "There's water—a pond or a lake?"

"Clear sky? Clouds?"

"Slow-moving clouds reflected in the water." I opened my eyes.

Jean smiled. "Play it."

When I finished, he clapped softly. "Slow-moving clouds, still water. All there, Dana. Just right."

The pond I imagined wasn't a pond I'd plucked from the gallery of ponds I knew. That wasn't the point. The effect of cloud reflections in the water's calm surface was. These were in the music. Now they were in me.

"What about the Schubert?" Jean flipped through the score and smoothed it open.

"Sometimes, I feel like I'm in a maze. I get lost in the repeats."

"I hear that when you play it."

"What do you mean?"

"You're tentative, holding back, as if you're feeling your way. But, you know, you need to trust yourself more. You said it yourself: You know the notes. Now, tell the story."

"I don't understand."

Jean motioned me over to the couch, spread the score across his lap and leaned back, his legs stretched out under the coffee table. "Schubert marks the score in all the usual ways—tempo, dynamics, phrasing. That's the easy part. The hard part? This is a theme and five variations. It's like having five different perspectives on a beautiful landscape. Pretend you're a movie director. This is the opening shot of your film. You move from a bird's-eye view to a close-up in the sunlight, to a middle-distance view as the clouds pass, and so forth.

"I'll try that. Maybe that will help me with some of the problems."

"Technical?"

"Sometimes I feel like I'm losing control."

"Which part do you like best?"

"The fifth variation."

Jean nodded. "Why?"

"It's fun." I laughed. "And it's the last one."

"Before you begin, remember that. It's a kind of homecoming." He placed his hand palm down on the score, his eyes holding mine, as if that way he could transfer to me the feelings he described so that I would feel them and convey them in my own playing. "One more thing. Every time you perform, you're meeting the audience for the first time. This Impromptu is a gift, a wonderful surprise. It's your job to unwrap it and dazzle them with what's inside."

The difference between his method and Mademoiselle's couldn't have been clearer. Mademoiselle emphasized mastery and control. Jean showed me how to make the music mine.

"You have it all, Dana"—he took and held my right hand, palm up, gently stroking it with his index finger— "here." He kissed my forehead. "And here."

o o o

One morning in early August, Jean sat next to me, working with me on a new fingering for a passage in the Schubert. I tried it out. It was like untying a tricky knot. Jean touched my arm. I looked up. Mom was standing across the room. In the mirror on the wall behind her, I could see Jean and me, side by side, framed by the open lid of the piano. I hadn't heard the car, hadn't heard the kitchen screen door slam. Why was she here? She usually didn't arrive home until later in the afternoon. For all these weeks, I had simply taken for granted that Jean and I could work together, uninterrupted. This was my time. Mom was at work. She had her own schedule. Here, now, she was an intruder.

Jean started to get up. I shook my head. He sat down.

"Come with me, Dana," Mom said, her voice low and tight.

I checked the clock on the bookcase. "We're almost done, Mom."

"Now, Dana."

I shook my head. "When I finish." She left the room.

I played the passage again, up to speed with the new fingering, flawlessly. Twenty minutes later, Jean left.

Mom sat at the kitchen table, staring into space, holding a cup of coffee. "How long has this been going on?"

"All summer."

"Every day?"

"Almost."

"Why haven't you told us?"

"Because I knew you'd object."

She went to the sink, turned the faucet on. And off. She leaned against the counter, facing me, hands in her pockets. "You're here alone. We don't know this boy or anything about him."

"I told you everything you need to know the first time you met him. He studies piano and conducting at NEC. Maybe you don't re-member because you were paying more attention to the color of his skin and his tattoo."

Mom's eyes widened. She shook her head. "No, Dana. I didn't know."

"Because you weren't listening. He's a pianist, a good one. He has helped me every day this summer."

"A pianist, then. How is he helping you?"

"If you promise not to interrupt, I'll explain."

"I'm listening."

"Today, for instance, he showed me fingering that works much better for me in the Schubert."

She raised her eyebrows. Mademoiselle taught me the fingering she had learned, fingering passed down generation to generation. To change it was like denying God.

"And how to prevent wrist cramp." Mademoiselle's remedy? More slow practice. Which didn't solve the problem. "He showed me how to shift the weight of my arm off my wrist. That worked."

Mom nodded. Even she understood this. Then, "What will you tell Mademoiselle?"

"I hope she hears the improvement."

The sound of the surf, the birds in the garden, all the usual reminders of early afternoon pooled around us.

"So that's it?"

"That's it?"

"Between you and your friend?"

"Jean, you mean?"

She pursed her lips. "Jean, yes."

"Yes, Mom, that's it, really."

I tried to see myself as she saw me: growing up, making my own decisions. I hoped she realized she could let me go, that I wasn't Lil. I wasn't rebelling; I was trying to do my best. Thanks to Jean's coaching, I thought I had at least a chance to place second or third in the competition.

o o o

Once I had the pieces in my fingers, under control, the glitches smoothed out, Jean and I worked on my memory. During the last two weeks of August, he tested me, stopping me in mid-phrase, talking to me to distract me, then having me pick up where I left off. At first, I stumbled around, got lost, backtracked to find my place. Eventually, no matter where he stopped me, I could carry on.

I no longer feared the competition. And I didn't care if Jimmy Bauer won. I just wanted to play as well as I knew I could.

I met Jean at Joe's on Friday of Labor Day weekend, my last day at the library, a couple of hours before his last gig. We sat on the bench across the street, watching a few wind surfers making the most of the light breeze.

He handed me a small, flat package wrapped in crinkly silver paper, tied with a blue ribbon. "You can open it now, if you want."

It was a CD in a blank jewel case.

"The guys and I made it for you. Our favorite tunes—zydeco, that is—whenever you need some sunshine." He touched my cheek. "Call me sometime."

We didn't make any promises. Or say goodbye.

o o o

The night before the competition, my parents were out for dinner with friends. I called Jean in Boston to tell him as much as I knew, so far, about the next day.

"How many of you?" he asked.

"Eight. Four in the morning, four after lunch."

"When's your turn?"

"Right after lunch—which I'm not planning to eat, by the way."

"What will you do in the morning?"

"Read the scores over, then warm up."

"And the butterflies?"

"Swarming."

He chuckled. "Remember what I said."

"Everything?"

"Remember to breathe, wise guy."

"That's my favorite part."

"What do you mean?"

"It's the only part that always works."

"Knock 'em out, Dana." His low, quiet tone held out to me all the energy and focus we'd built together over the summer.

Whatever was unfinished between us would remain unfinished. I didn't know if I'd see him again. He'd said he might come back to Joe's the next summer, but that would depend on his course work. There were summer school courses he could take, especially if he found a gig in Boston. He wanted to graduate early, to prepare for a conducting competition. It was as if, like a piece of music transposed to a different key, we had transposed our relationship during our summer of working together. He might have become my boyfriend; instead, he had been my coach. And that was just fine.

Inhale as the adrenaline surges; exhale to let it go. Every day I had practiced this technique with Jean in the series of "startle" tests he dreamed up to condition me to handle my fight-or-flight reaction. These worked nearly every time. With practice, my hands and legs didn't tremble, my heart didn't pound, my throat didn't close.

o o o

At the piano, I bowed to the four judges seated in the second row. The audience sat in the darkened auditorium behind them, invisible from the stage.

One of the judges, a woman, stood. "Good afternoon, Dana. We are looking forward to hearing you play Schubert's Impromptu, opus 142, no. 3. Please take as long as you need before you begin."

Wait 'til I tell Jean. I reached for the knobs to adjust the bench. My hands were so damp and cold, they kept slipping off. My pounding heart drowned out all other sound except Jean's voice in my ear:

"S'okay, Dana. Inhale. Exhale." I closed my eyes, heard the Impromptu's opening passage in my head, and began to play, listening to every note, shaping every phrase.

o o o

My problems with the Schubert began and ended with the repeats within each of the variations. The notes are the same, but the idea is to play them differently, different versions of the same material. Changes in emphasis help, as if you're saying to the listener, "Here it is again, only this time, please notice the lovely bass line. See? It's the mirror image of the treble."

Near the end of the fifth variation—six measures, eight measures? —as if I'd missed a step on my way down an unfamiliar stairway, my mind went blank. My hands, lay inert on the keyboard in front of me, detached and unresponsive. *Do something. Play something. Play anything.* Hadn't Mademoiselle warned me? *If you stop listening to yourself, you'll be lost.* So I played a chord, something that sounded more like Bartok than Schubert. I had come to the end of the Impromptu and lost my way. I needed then to get off the stage, to escape from the dark, from my failure, from the audience, which only then began to stir. Scattered applause followed me off the stage.

It was over.

Mom and Dad waited for me in the corridor backstage. Dad took my hand. "It's okay, Dana. Whatever happens, whatever the results, you did fine."

I'd had my chance. There would be no *da capo al fine.*

We went out to the lobby, where Mademoiselle joined us. "Next time, it will be different. You'll see." She patted my shoulder, looking past me at my parents.

Jimmy, the last to perform, came out, grinning. Juilliard had already accepted him, early decision. Winning the competition would be the icing on the cake.

Half an hour later, we gathered in the auditorium—competitors, family members, teachers, and supporters. The judge gave a short speech about what an honor it was to serve on the panel, how impressed the judges were with our commitment and talent. "And now, it gives me great pleasure to announce our four winners. In fourth place, Ella Jenkins. In third place, Ross Michaels. In second place, Alice Anderson. And in first place, Jimmy Bauer."

I closed my eyes, imagining how I'd feel had I been awarded a ribbon, or even an honorable mention. Dad hugged me and whispered. "You'll have another chance next year, sweetheart."

○ ○ ○

Dad, Mom, and I went out to dinner at the Crow's Nest and sat on the deck overlooking the harbor. Everything, even the flourless chocolate cake, my favorite, tasted like sawdust. When the bottle of Veuve Clicquot arrived, Dad asked the waiter to pour three glasses and lifted his in a toast. He set it down, folded his hands in front of him on the table. "So, honey, what do you think happened?"

I shook my head. "It felt like when the phone goes dead." When I closed my eyes, I could still see my hands, the hands of a stranger, lying on the keyboard, white, helpless, still.

Mom and Dad exchanged a look. "We'll talk more later, Dana," Mom said.

○ ○ ○

"Dana?"

I held my breath. My door was closed. Maybe she'd go away. I didn't want to talk. I needed time, settling time, to get used to "after." "Before" was over.

She opened the door. "Dana? Sweetie?"

"What, Mom?" I sat up and switched on the lamp.

She sat in the armchair across from my bed, sniffling. "A story about your grandmother. I want to tell you." She held one of my dad's handkerchiefs in her right hand, bunched against her chest. In her left, she held the photograph of my grandmother.

"Why are you crying?"

"You know that Mama stopped playing when Lil was born." She blew her nose. "There's more to the story."

She took a deep breath and cleared her throat. "Before she got pregnant with Lil, Mama had begun to work on a recital, her first public solo performance in several years. It was hard for her to play after she got pregnant, but she didn't let up until she had to." Mom laughed softly. "Her belly got in the way." Mom smoothed and folded the handkerchief in her lap. "Then, Lil came. She was a breech baby."

"A breech baby?"

"Born bottom first. They had to do a caesarean."

Lil, my footloose, fancy-free aunt, nearly hadn't made it. On the dresser, I had a photo of Lil and me at the beach. In a wide-brimmed sun hat, her blond hair blowing around her bare shoulders, laughing, she glows. Her energy flows into the room.

"Papa talked her into postponing the recital for three months. The night of her performance, I wore a white organdy dress with a green sash. I can still remember the sound and feel of it, how it swished against my legs." She smiled. "It tickled something awful when I walked."

Mom held out the photograph of my grandmother.

I imagined the scene, the rustle of the audience settling, my grandmother in her blue velvet gown.

"In the middle of the first piece on her program, a Bach partita, she stopped, pushed back from the piano, and collapsed onto the keyboard. I thought she had died."

Mom took a deep breath, as if preparing herself for the last push up a steep hill. "She had a breakdown, Dana. Eventually she was hospitalized."

"Why Mom? What was wrong with her?"

"Depression. Chronic depression." Mom's voice caught. "They call it dysthymia now. She never played again."

o o o

Several weeks later, Mademoiselle reassured me that every soloist had memory lapses from time to time. It was just nerves, she said. I would learn how to improvise so that when—or if—it happened again, I would be able to find my way back and continue from where I had left off.

"Still," she added, "the best way to limit these lapses is to play as often as possible for others—your friends and relatives, your parents and their friends. You'll soon be able to relax and enjoy your gift, the gift you're giving to others."

I didn't tell her there wouldn't be a next time, that I had decided I would play the piano only when I wanted to, that I wouldn't apply to the conservatory or compete, ever again.

o o o

At the beginning of my senior year, my best friend Anne and her family moved to California. The day the movers came, she rode her bike over to our house to say goodbye. Her bike, a ten-speed Schwinn, was nearly new. I'd been saving baby-sitting money to buy one like it.

We'd promised to write and call one another. Now, I tried to joke. "I sure hope you'll find someone to help you with your math homework, someone as patient as me, I mean."

"You're just envious I'm going to learn to surf." We laughed.

"Maybe you can show me how when you come out here next summer." I had invited her to stay with us the week of the Fourth of July. We were still waiting for our parents to agree and sort out the details.

By this time, it was clear that neither of us wanted to say goodbye. "See ya later, alligator."

"In a while, crocodile," Anne replied.

Neither of us moved. We both began to laugh, until we were laughing so hard, we were crying.

"I'm going in now," I said.

"I'm leaving." Anne didn't move.

"What's wrong?" I asked.

"Don't you want your going-away present?"

"What going-away present?"

She disengaged her kickstand and set her bike there at the edge of the sidewalk. "She's all yours, Dana."

"What are you talking about?"

"I asked my dad. He agreed I could give it to you. He talked to your dad. He agreed, too. It's yours, Dana."

I remembered how much I'd wanted the green Schwinn years ago, how I'd feigned happiness for the gift of my grandmother's piano. Now, I released the kickstand, mounted the bike, and rode it up the street.

Anne ran along beside me, yelling, "You go girl!"

o o o

At the end of my senior year, I told Mademoiselle and my parents that I wanted to major in journalism in college, that I wasn't sure if I would continue piano lessons. Instead, I'd focus on the journalism courses that would prepare me to work for a magazine or newspaper after graduation.

Later, I overheard my parents talking about my decision. In tears, Mom said, "I wanted her to play the piano for Mama."

Dad didn't say anything for a while. Then, "Dana isn't your mother, Grace. Just like you and Lil, she'll find her own way."

After college, I played the piano once in a while, as if visiting a place I'd loved and believed lost. It wasn't lost; it had been waiting for me all along, waiting for me to return to it on my own terms.

Tom

Summer 1997

"Where's the lake, Dad?" Ben locks eyes with Matt in the rearview mirror.

"See that dead pine tree up there on the left? The lake's just around the bend." Matt catches Ben's eye in the rearview mirror. He winks. Ben winks back.

"Just around the bend. Check," Ben murmurs.

Matt slows and rolls down his window. "Smell that?"

Ben inhales noisily. "Sure smells like hay."

Grace laughs.

Next to Ben in the backseat, behind Grace, Tom rolls his eyes.

Matt pulls over. "There she is."

"That's the lake all right." Both boys, heads together, shoulder to shoulder, lean over the front seat. Just ahead, on the right side of the road, a low sign, green lettering on a white background, announces "Camp Overlook." Matt pulls over next to it.

Beyond the post-and-rail fence, a meadow slopes down to a stand of birches and white spruce. A narrow gap marks the beginning of a trail through the trees to Camp Overlook's parking area, its administration building, and clusters of cabins. Like steppingstones, the cabins occupy clearings in the woods across the broad ridge of the peninsula that ends at Jackson's Point on the lake. Beyond the point, Lake Champlain gleams, its wind-ruffled surface sapphire blue flecked with whitecaps.

"Two years ago, you said it's as big as Narragansett Bay, remember?" Ben leans over the seat, his left hand on Matt's shoulder.

"Sure do. And it is. It is as big—as wide as the bay, I mean."

"I looked it up."

"And?" Matt smiles.

"It's longer and wider than the bay, Dad." Ben's voice rises triumphantly on "and."

"I stand corrected, Your Honor."

Matt rolls the window down and pulls back onto the road. He inhales the sweet smell of new-mown hay, remembering his three summers at Camp Overlook—sailing in his first race, the wind and spray on his face; the sweet tang of burning maple wood and the boys singing around the campfire, the thrill of being dragged up and out of the water by the ski boat his first time on water-skis. Twenty-five years ago. *Yesterday.*

Today, cars, kids, and harried parents crowd the camp's parking lot. Matt points to the main building, a rectangular, clapboard, two-story structure housing the director's office, the infirmary, and the canteen, which doubles as post office. "Looks like they painted it," he says.

"The shutters, anyway," Grace murmurs.

"Remember the first time, when I thought the canteen was a 'canteen,' you know, like the one you put water in?" Ben leans over Matt's left shoulder. "How weird was that?"

"It was weird, all right," Tom circles his finger around, shaking his head.

"Then I went there and found the postcards and stamps, like you told me, Dad."

"And the candy counter," Tom adds.

"There." Matt noses the car between a Jeep and a VW van and warns them not to bump them as they unpack.

The night before, Matt had checked off each item on their lists as Tom and Ben packed their duffle bags: shirts, shorts, socks, shoes, jackets, sweaters, bathing trunks, and towels, everything tagged and accounted for. Ben had packed his watercolors, pencils, and sketchpads in the carrying case Grace had given him and placed it on top of his clothes before closing the duffle.

"It's hard to believe this is Ben's third summer," Matt told Grace later. "As soon as we zipped the bags, I thought back to the first year. He sat on his bed, watching me pack. He seemed so alone. I had second thoughts, nearly got cold feet, remember?"

"Yesterday, he told me he was glad to be going back, that he didn't know what he would do with himself if we told him he had to stay home this year," Grace said. "He'll never be Tom. But one is enough, don't you agree?"

Matt raised his hand. "I second the motion."

o o o

That morning, as soon as they turned north onto I95, Ben had leaned forward, elbows propped on the back of the front seat. "I wonder if they got rid of that weird broccoli. Creamed broccoli? Yuck!" He shuddered.

Matt glanced at Ben. "Maybe this year, they'll serve breakfast in bed."

Ben scoffed. "This is camp, Dad, remember?"

Tom held out a paper bag, "Hey, Ben." Ben reached into the bag and pulled out a box of Raisinets.

"Thanks, man." Ben opened the box and offered it to Tom.

Tom shook his head, "All yours."

o o o

On Sunday afternoon, a week later, the trumpet flourish blaring from the camp loudspeaker announces the beginning of rest period. Ben ducks into the bathhouse, into the last shower stall, where he hides, waiting for the all-clear—the sound of the cabin door closing behind Pete on his way to the counselors' weekly meeting.

His first summer, he'd found the trail one afternoon when he snuck out for a walk instead of playing cards or reading in his cabin. They had been warned not to go beyond the boundary markers, signs that read, "Never Alone, Never Roam."

"What if we do?" a boy asked.

"They'll send you home."

Ben had looked around. No boundary markers in sight here. Besides, the trail was well-worn. So he couldn't get lost, could he? That first afternoon, he had followed it out to Jackson's Point, where he found the granite boulder on the edge of the cliff. On a clear day, you felt you could reach out and touch the Adirondacks, to the west across the lake. Sometimes, lying in his bunk at night, he closed his eyes and followed the mountains' ridgeline, imagining drawing the scene, imagining the sky above them filled with billowing clouds.

He had three sketchbooks, one from each of the two previous summers, with his drawings of the lake and the Adirondacks, the camp's harbor and cobblestone beach, each one signed and dated. This summer, in the third sketchbook, brand new, he plans to draw the cloudscapes that form over the mountains and the lake most afternoons.

He heads for Jackson's Point, passing familiar trail markers—a downed paper birch, its trunk riddled with borer holes, the remains of a hunter's blind perched on a flimsy wood support, collapsing under its own weight.

"I'm back," he shouts, startling a pheasant into flight to the left of the trail ahead of him. The bird veers right, toward the deep woods, away from the cliff, away from the lake.

Ben steps into the clearing at the edge of the cliff, its rough pebbled surface strewn with twigs and pinecones. There, facing the lake, the eight-foot tall, slump-shouldered granite boulder stands guard at the edge of a grove of weather-beaten pines. He runs his hand over the familiar sun-warmed surface, absorbing its welcome. "I'm back," he says. "I could tell you some stories. Wish you could tell me yours."

Pencil in hand, poised over the sketchbook in his lap, he sits, settling against the boulder, taking in the pinecones and a crow feather lying in front of him. He sketches these objects, their dark pockets and highlights, in quick, sure strokes, attentive to shape and size, the space between them, the surface shadows and the shadows each one casts on the soil around it. He closes his eyes. Opens them. Looks up and out over the lake, at the rumpled cloud cover that stretches nearly from shore to shore.

o o o

Closely packed like fish scales, the small clouds hover over a lone sailboat heading northwest. A mackerel sky. Ben knows it signals the approach of stormy weather. Will the boat reach the far side of the lake before the storm breaks? The skipper leans out over the water, his silhouette rising and falling above the whitecaps. When the wind begins to shift, the boat comes about, tacking to the northeast, its bow wave sending billows of spray into the blue. Hunkered down in the cockpit, the sailor leans forward, steadying the tiller.

Ben sketches the cloud cover, the boat, and the in-bound whitecaps, spewing spindrift. He pulls his sweatshirt over his knees and tucks his head into the hood, shielding his eyes and ears against the burst of lightning across the lake and the crack of thunder that follows.

The wind plummets into silence. For a moment, it's so still, Ben can hear the drone of the tractor down at camp. Then, as if shot from a water cannon, a stinging spray of wind-driven rain and hail, twigs and needles, batters him. He shields his eyes, squints at the sailboat.

A hundred yards offshore, the surging waves lift and rock it. Its sails begin to flap and flutter as it loses headway. The skipper's hood, a smudge of orange, glows dully through the spume.

Ben wipes the rain from his eyes and peers at the sailor through the downpour. The orange hood. Tom's Giants' hoodie. Ben scrambles to his feet. Shouts. He can't hear his own voice over the roaring in his ears. He shouts again. "Tom! Tommy!"

o o o

After lunch, as soon as his cabinmates settle in the dining hall to watch reruns of the World Cup quarter finals, Tom tells them he's going back to the cabin to study for his water safety instructor test.

"You crazy, man?"

"World Cup reruns?" He fake-yawns. Outside, he looks back once. No one is watching him. He heads down to the harbor the long way, keeping the administration building between him and the dining hall.

At the dock, he kneels on the far side of the boat locker, pulls on the life jacket, and drags out the sail bag for *Sunburst,* a Rhodes 19.

Tied up at the end of the dock, *Sunburst* beckons. Easy out, easy in. On Narragansett Bay, Tom has sailed larger boats single-handed. He can handle the 19-foot Rhodes. Especially on a day like today. Slight overcast—a light mackerel sky—a fifteen-knot breeze. He figures the rain won't start until he's on his way back. Coiling the sheets as he rigs the boat, he raises the jib, rocks back on his heels in the cockpit, and slings his arm over the tiller. Still, no one in sight. Loud cheering from the dining hall. The first match is off to a fast start.

He is, too.

He tightens and ties the laces of his hoodie as he clears the mouth of the harbor and rounds Jackson's Point, bracing himself, his back toward shore. Out on the open water, as soon as he raises the main, the strengthening wind grabs and fills it. He checks the time. He has two hours, maybe three, out and back, max. He snugs his hoodie again, zips the life jacket, and trims the sails. Knifing through the water, the bow wave curling high and even, the hull vibrates. *Sunburst* heels to port and Tom grips the tiller in both hands, his feet steadied against the cockpit.

Tom had tried to describe the thrill of sailing close-hauled. He could talk about finding and holding a position in the wind, how, if you got it just right, the ride felt effortless, the way skiing feels when you get close to the fall line. You knew that edge was where you had to be. The wind was like gravity. You had to feel it, to know how close to the edge you could get. Still, words were a poor substitute.

Tom comes about and sets the boat on a starboard tack heading northeast. If he can, he'll make run for it later, straight down the middle of the lake back to camp. He checks the time again. He's been out for a little over half an hour. Plenty of time to get back to camp before the end of the reruns. No one will be the wiser. Sweet. There was nothing like sailing solo, nothing like working the wind to take the boat to its top speed—alone. You, the wind, and the boat. You were in charge.

As soon as the boat settles, he feels the change in the wind. Cooler, sharper. He blinks and wipes the spray out of his eyes. He looks up at the telltale, notices the change in the cloud cover. It has thickened into dark swathes rolling southeast over the lake. To the north, a dark, anvil-shaped cloud looms, granular and sooty. Tom recognizes the storm warning, feels the boat respond as the wind picks up. Choppy now, the waves crest, frothy, uneven. Slapping down into the troughs, *Sunburst* shudders and hesitates before thrusting ahead up the face of the next wave.

Tom looks southeast toward camp. As he left the harbor, he'd noticed a fishing boat, a Boston Whaler, moored in the adjacent cove. It's gone now. Probably on its way home.

He hears them before he sees them: A flock of gulls flying toward Jackson's Point and the shelter of the cove.

The sudden chill convinces him to come about and head west again, toward the middle of the lake. Moving south, the storm is riding a strong northerly. If he catches it just right, he'll have a quick, straight run back to camp. The boat seems to sense his urgency. The telltale chatters, the halyards snap as he races to stay ahead of it.

The tiller tucked tight between his arm and his chest, Tom pays out the sheets, easing the jib and the main until they billow side by side in wing-on-wing position for his run south.

The jib bellies and hums; the main fills. Drenched and shivering, his hands slipping on the sodden sheets, Tom slumps into the cockpit, anticipating the moment of calm when the boat settles into its homeward run. Instead, a squall, gritty with hail, grabs and sucks at the sails like a powerful drain.

He'll have to ride out the storm. He begins to lower the main to reef it, but the halyard jams in the middle of the mast. He shakes the sheet, jiggles the boom, to no effect. He cleats the boom, ducking his head low against the torrent, stumbling over the sheets piled in the cockpit. He can hear Johnny, "Tidy up those sheets, boys, else you'll get tangled up when you least expect it." He kicks the sheets against the side of the boat, the best he can do for now, clambers up on the foredeck, and crawls toward the mast. The squeal of tearing metal follows a loud pop. The boat begins to slew as the mast buckles. The sail collapses.

The boom swings free, knocking him overboard.

o o o

Under water, his lungs aching, he strains to get his bearings. He kicks once, twice, up to the surface, and bumps into the sail, now filling with water. He can't lift his head or his arms. *Breathe!* The frigid water sucks at him. He feels pressure around his right ankle. He reaches down. Feels the sheet looped around it. Pinned under the sail, tangled in the sheet—must be one of the jib sheets, he thinks—he's trapped in a shallow air pocket.

With each lurch of the hull, the sheet tightens, the air pocket shrinks.

o o o

Lashed by the wind, the pines at the cliff's edge twist and sway around Ben, bending nearly double. In a sudden gust, the top of the tree snaps off and tumbles down the cliff face. At that moment, like a mirror image, the mast topples. Tom disappears. The orange hood vanishes.

Rising and falling in the surf, at the mercy of the gusting wind, the sailboat continues to drift offshore. *Where is Tom? He'll make it back, won't he?*

Ben stuffs his sketchpad and pencils into his daypack. *Who gave you permission to take the boat out? I bet you didn't ask. It's only the first week of camp. Did you really think you wouldn't get caught? Wait 'til Dad finds out. He'll ground you for a year. You're such a jerk, Tommy!*

"Where the hell are you, Tom?" The wind tears the words from his mouth, swallowing them whole.

Ben staggers back through the woods, slipping on pine needles, tripping over roots and fallen branches. The dining hall is dark and empty—power failure? —the boathouse, deserted. He huddles next to the sail locker, shivering.

Where is everyone?

o o o

A breaking wave slams him against the boat. Scissor-kicking to keep his head in the air pocket, he feels his right shoe fall off. Maybe now he can loosen the sheet. He ducks under again, wedging his thumbs between the sheet and his ankle, straining to slide it off. Just when it seems his lungs will explode, the sheet slackens. He forces his fingers around it, pulling and pushing at it until it releases. Numbness gives way to searing pain.

Back in the pocket, he swallows water with his first gulp of air, coughs it up. He can't feel his hands. He kicks and dog paddles toward the sail's edge, maybe eight feet away, pushes his right fist up against it to make an air pocket, takes a deep breath. Blacks out.

When he comes to, a swimmer has him in a cross-chest carry in open water, moving away from the Rhodes. "Just a little farther now. Let me do the work." The man's tone is calm and conversational, but he's breathing hard. They reach the stern of a Boston Whaler, and the man grabs on with his free hand. Tom reaches for the gunwale, but his fingers are too numb to grip it. He tries again with both hands and holds on.

The man scrambles over the side into the stern and grasps Tom under the arms. "Now, son!" Tom's left shoulder takes the brunt of his fall into the cockpit.

His rescuer sags down next to him, coughing and spitting. He's about his dad's age, Tom thinks, husky, like a body builder. "Name's Pete," the man says, "Pete Jackson. Guess you got hit hard out there. You from Overlook?"

Head down, Tom nods.

Pete rummages in the Whaler's locker and hands Tom a towel and a sleeping bag. "This'll have to do."

Tom strips off his hoodie and towels off. His right ankle is bleeding; he's lost his left shoe, too. He wraps the sleeping bag around him, zips it up to his neck, and slumps onto the bench.

Pete pulls an oilskin on over his wetsuit, starts the engine, and weighs anchor. Turning downwind, the Whaler bucks, growling and digging in as it crosses the turbulent surface.

Sunburst's hull and damaged rigging appear and disappear in the swells. A jagged lightning flash pulses through the sky, now an oily green, followed by a crack of thunder that reverberates through the boat and across the lake. The whistling wind nearly drowns out the Whaler's laboring motor.

The four-foot swells out of the northwest lift and push the boat south. Legs spread, feet braced, Pete strains to hold it steady. The Whaler could capsize if it stalls and gets swamped. Every time the bow dips, Tom's breath catches, his body holding the memory of the water around and over him under the sail. To the east, the granite face of Jackson's Point gleams yellow in the hazy light. Behind them, to the northeast, the sky has begun to clear.

Pete calls over his shoulder, "Almost missed you. I thought maybe you'd swum to shore." He adjusts the throttle and gestures at the hoodie. "That saved your life."

Tom looks down at the sodden hoodie on the deck. "I was wrong about the weather."

"Can't be certain what you'll find out here, no matter what the weatherman tells you. Well, if Johnny lets you solo, you must know a thing or two." Pete glances at him.

He knows, Tom realizes. He knows I'm AWOL. "I didn't expect the storm so soon. Mackerel sky, you know, I thought I had two, three hours."

Pete nods, smiles. "On this lake, with these mountains, you can't be sure. Best to plan for the worst. That's why I tucked into that little cove, just around the corner from the camp. You picked the right boat, though. That Rhodes, she's like a life-preserver with sails. Not much speed, of course, but safe as houses." He smiles down at Tom. "When he finishes reading you the riot act, ask Johnny about the time we got caught out here in his dad's fishing boat, struck by lightning." Pete laughs and shakes his head. He doesn't talk about the mast.

Tom pulls the sleeping bag tighter. Should he tell Pete about the halyard? About what he'd been trying to do? What he knew how to do? If he'd been able to reef the main, he could have ridden out the storm, maybe made it back to camp before anyone knew he'd been gone.

"This your first week back?"

Tom nods. Would Johnny ground him for the summer? Send him home? For sure Mac would call his parents. And expect them to pay for the repairs. What happened, anyway? Tom had practiced reefing the mainsail plenty of times. What had he done wrong?

As the Whaler rounds Jackson's Point and enters the camp harbor, Pete says, "I've known Johnny since we were kids. Good sailor." He adjusts his grip on the wheel and looks at Tom. "We had some wild times. Johnny knows plenty of stories." Pete winks and grins. "So do I."

Tom pulls his arms out of the sleeping bag and straightens up. "Is the boat okay?" His voice sounds hollow, as if he were speaking through a cardboard tube. Up ahead, near the dining hall, a few guys take turns dribbling a soccer ball, jostling one another for control.

"Probably. But the mast is kaput. Johnny will figure out what happened and check the others. The whole fleet is about the same age. Time to sort them out, I guess."

So maybe it wasn't his fault, Tom thinks. Maybe there was something wrong with the boat? That wouldn't get him off the hook. Still, if it turned out the mast wasn't sound, he would know his reefing technique wasn't to blame.

Small comfort.

o o o

The clearing sky, a pale gold wash flecked with feathery clouds, promises a fine sunset. Pete ties up at the end of the dock in *Sunburst's* berth. Tom drops the towel, unzips the sleeping bag, and picks up his hoodie.

"Son of a gun." Pete grabs the towel, kneels, and presses it against Tom's oozing ankle.

"The nurse will have to see to this," he says. "My first aid kit went walkabout." He laughs. "Like you."

With Pete's help, Tom makes it over the side of the Whaler onto the dock.

Weight on his left foot, he hops along, his right hand on Pete's shoulder.

"Hey, Tom! Where you been?" one of the soccer players yells.

Tom waves and keeps walking.

"Time to face the music." Pete nods up the hill behind the boat house, where Johnny stands on the steps of the infirmary.

"That storm came straight out of nowhere," Pete tells Johnny. "One of your 19s capsized. The mast went."

"Looks like you had quite a time, fella." Johnny says. He looks down at Tom's ankle. He glances at Pete, then Tom, "What in hell got into you, Carlson? You broke every rule in the book." He looks again the ankle. "We'll sort this out later."

"Yes, sir," Tom says.

"First, the nurse'll fix you up and you can check on your brother."

"Check on him where?"

"Infirmary." Johnny nods up the steps.

"What happened?"

"You'll have to ask him yourself. Do you need help up the steps?"

"No, sir."

Johnny and Pete head back down to the dock. "…reminds me of me," Pete says.

Johnny scoffs. "Me, too."

o o o

There are two single beds in the room. Ben's sketchbook lies on the bedside table between them. Warned by the nurse not to wake Ben, Tom tiptoes over and picks up the sketchbook. The first drawing shows a mackerel sky over the lake, cumulus clouds looming to the north, a lone sailboat on a port tack, the skipper obscured by the spray. Today's date and Ben's initials are scrawled in the lower right-hand corner. Still damp from the storm, the paper's edges have begun to curl.

Ben's eyelids flutter. His freckles stand out, dark as cinders against the white pillowcase.

Tom leans over him. "Hey, Ben." The door opens behind him.

"What's not to understand about 'do not wake your brother,' Tom? Haven't you two broken enough rules today?" Janine, the camp nurse, comes in with an electric blanket.

Tom limps across the room to the chair by the window.

"He needs sleep." Janine shakes her head. "You boys. What a way to start the summer." She spreads the blanket over Ben and plugs it in. At the door, she turns to Tom, her eyes softening. "He'll be fine, Tom."

Tom removes the pillow behind him in the chair, drops it on the floor in front of him, and gingerly lifts his foot onto it. His bandaged ankle throbs. No stitches, at least. His head is okay. Just a bruise.

"What happened?" Ben's teeth chatter. His voice is hoarse.

Tom gets up. Limps over to the bed. "Everybody seems to know what happened to me. You're the mystery. You've got hypothermia. How did that happen?" Tom flicks a piece of lint off the blanket. He holds up the drawing. "You were AWOL, too?"

Ben flushes. "Not like you," he says. "I watched you go overboard. And disappear. I thought you drowned." His voice cracks. "Serve you right."

"What about you?" Tom retorts. "How come they found you down at the boathouse, anyway?"

"When I saw you go over, I ran back for help." Ben stares across the room. His lips quiver, then tighten. He looks up at Tom. "I couldn't find anyone. I decided to wait. I thought maybe you'd swim back. I must have passed out."

"How did you know it was me?"

"Your orange hoodie. What do you think?" Ben pushes himself

up, eyes wide, bright with tears. "Screw you, Tom. You don't care what happens. To you or anyone else." He sags back, panting.

"Don't blame me for what happened to you. I didn't make you go out there."

"Jerk." Ben pulls the covers over his head.

Later, sitting in the chair, listening to Ben's deep, even breathing, Tom thinks again about all the times he had practiced reefing the mainsail. What was the point of practicing if the one time you need it, the maneuver didn't work? It wasn't his fault the sail stuck. And Ben was wrong. He did care.

He and Ben weren't much alike, really. But both believed in practicing to get something right. This was Dad's idea. And it worked. Except today. They'd both been in the wrong, both caught out. Would Mac send them both home? And Dad and Mom? What would they do? They couldn't blame him for what happened to Ben. And he sure wasn't to blame for the problem with the sail.

Sure, they could bawl him out for taking the boat without permission. But the wrecked mast? What if one of the junior kids had taken the boat out and the sail had collapsed? Even with a counselor onboard, the kids would have panicked; it would have been a mess.

Tom chuckled. Even he knew he was rationalizing. Even he understood he had been in the wrong. There was no excuse.

o o o

In the middle of the night, Tom wakes in the chair. He shuffles over and gets into the bed next to Ben's.

"You're a dickhead." Ben's voice is hoarse.

"Yeah?"

"What were you trying to prove, anyway?"

Tom props himself on his elbow. "Seriously? That storm? How was I supposed to know the mast would break? That the boat would capsize on me?"

"It was like you vanished. Into thin air." Ben snaps his fingers. He rubs his hands over his eyes.

Tom watches Ben's eyes. "Things didn't work out too good for you, either."

"I've never been so cold, not even that time it was 30 below and we skied anyway." Ben sniffles "You're a dork. I hope Dad makes you pay for the damn boat."

"The mast, anyway," Tom says.

"Do you think they'll send us home?"

"Me, maybe. Not you."

"I won't stay if you go home."

Tom laughs softly. "Not sure either of us has much to say about it, one way or the other. We'll find out tomorrow, probably."

Ben rolls over on his side. "Still got your Giants cap?"

"You want it?"

Ben's eyes smile.

"It's yours."

"You mean it?"

"If you give me the drawing."

Ben nods.

"I'll never forget that feeling." Tom swallows hard. "I was flying."

o o o

Tom wakes before seven. Snoring lightly, Ben lies spread-eagled on the other bed, the heating blanket on the floor. Tom rolls over and sits up. He pushes himself off the bed, gingerly putting his weight down. His ankle aches but holds steady.

From the window he can see *Sunburst*, the mast lashed to the deck, tied up at the end of the dock, bobbing in its own reflection under the cloudless sky. Below him, just beyond the infirmary steps, the lawn slopes to the lake. Side by side, four dark green Adirondack chairs lie upside down where the lawn meets the cobble beach, safe now, clear of the storm. *Kicking their legs in the air*, Tom laughs. Across the room behind him, the door opens.

"Good morning, boys."

He turns.

Ben sits up. "Dad? What are you doing here? Mom?"

Grace goes to the bed and sits beside him, holding him, rocking him back and forth. Her breath catches. She shakes her head. "Mac called us yesterday afternoon. He told us what happened, that you were both okay. We wanted to see for ourselves." She looks at Tom. "Really, Tommy? What were you thinking?"

Matt clears his throat. "We'll have a talk about that later. First, breakfast. Then we'll meet with Mac to find out what happens now." He and Mac had been friends since their first summer at Overlook. They had sailed together, won the tennis doubles trophy, and stayed in touch over the years. Mac was a math teacher. He'd taken the summer job as camp director fifteen years ago.

"What do you mean?" Tom asks.

"The mast, for starters."

"What else?"

"Possibly some structural damage to the deck. But we won't know that until the boatyard crew look at it."

"Oh." Tom looks down at the floor.

"The most important thing is that you're okay. We can deal with the repairs," Grace says.

"What about me?" Ben stares at the three of them, blinking back tears.

"You were both out of line," Matt says. "Tom could have drowned; you could have slipped and fallen from the cliff. Mac can't let you off the hook for breaking the rules. It's up to him." He looks at Grace, still sitting beside Ben, her head lowered.

Matt checks his watch. "It's eight. We're supposed to meet Mac at nine in his office. Let's go get some breakfast."

o o o

At the diner on the main road, a couple of miles from camp, Ben pokes at his scrambled eggs and crumbles a piece of toast. Tom finishes Ben's eggs with his waffle. Grace and Matt each have cereal, toast, and coffee. No one speaks.

Back at camp, they head single file up the stairs to Mac's office. He greets them somberly, waves them over to the couch and armchairs facing his desk, pulls up a side chair and sits, facing them, a clipboard and pad in his lap.

Mac looks at Ben, sitting beside Grace on the couch, then at Tom, who has taken an armchair and sits across from Matt. Hands folded on the clipboard, a half-smile softening his serious look, he clears his throat. "So what's the plan for your second act?"

Ben and Tom look at one another.

Mac goes on, "I learned this morning that the Rhodes mast hadn't been properly stepped, so anyone sailing her would have been at risk of something like what happened to you, Tom." He looks at Matt. "So, we'll repair the boat and check all the others. Lesson learned."

He looks down at the clipboard, then continues, "Only one other time since I've been director did we finish our first week with a near catastrophe. Fifteen years ago, we had a horse who knew how to open the paddock gate. Which she did, late the first night. There was no moon. It was around midnight. She walked right out. Nineteen horses followed her down to the meadow, where they all stopped to graze. If she'd led them through the meadow into the woods and out to the Point …?" He shakes his head. "We installed a new latch. One she couldn't open."

Mac looks at Tom, then at Ben. "Your case is different. You both know the rules and you broke them. So, I have to come up with a punishment to fit the crime. Short of locking the two of you in your cabins whenever you have free time, I don't have a lot of options." He looked at Grace and Matt. "I could send you home, of course. Instead, I decided I'd like you to stay for the summer, as planned. I'm going to count on you to follow the rules. And if you step out of line again, well, I think you know the consequences." He clears his throat.

"The camp will pay to replace *Sunburst's* mast. Your Dad and Mom will pay for any other repairs.

"At our next assembly I am going to tell the others what you did and what happened to you. I'll also tell them what I've decided to do."

He turns to Tom. "For the rest of the summer, you'll manage the gear for all twelve sailboats, making sure everything is stored in each sail bag every day, and that the sail bags are locked up. If that had been the case yesterday, you wouldn't have been able to take the boat out. You'll do this under Johnny's supervision. And when you go out with the others, you'll be restricted to crew." He looks Tom in the eye. "Got that?"

Tom glances at Matt, who nods at Mac. "Yes, sir."

"As for you, Ben." Mac looks down at the pad in his lap. "I've seen your drawings. I know how much you enjoy sketching the lake and the mountains. I'm going to help you find a place where you can work, a safe place, that is. It won't be Jackson's Point, but it will be a place you'll like, I promise." Mac leans in, closer to Ben, so that Ben must look him in the eye. "If you ever go out to the Point, or anywhere else out of bounds, I'll send you home. Understood?"

Ben nods. Grace says, "Speak up, Ben."

"Yes, sir."

o o o

At the dock, looking over *Sunburst,* Matt checks the foredeck. "I don't get it," he tells Tom. "Something in the rigging must have snagged the halyard, so that the weight of the sail snapped the mast. A freak accident." He looked at Tom. "I remember we practiced together. I also remember it was a fine, light day. Too bad you got hit by that wind. Next time, you'll get it right."

"Because I'll do it sooner, you mean?"

"Better sooner than later." Matt smiles. "Call it a life lesson."

Ben

2006

On Friday afternoon after Ellie's last class, they drove to Pescadero, past fields of Brussels sprouts and Black Angus belly-deep in wild mustard and lupine. At four-thirty, just beyond Pigeon Point, they caught up with a flock of brown pelicans headed north, single file, hugging the coast. The fog bank hovering over the horizon earlier that afternoon now billowed above the surf line, eddying over the roadway in some places.

Ben flipped on the headlights. A cushion behind her head, Ellie drowsed in the passenger seat. She'd been up all night finishing her last paper. He reached over and touched her cheek.

She yawned and stretched. "How 'bout a story?"

"Have I told you about the time we rescued the pelican?"

"A brown pelican like the ones we see around the wharf?"

"Just like. That's a favorite hangout. Another is the Pescadero lagoon." Ben checked the rearview mirror. They'd reached the stretch of the road he liked best—a couple of miles north of Davenport, where it straightened out, smooth sailing, even in a dense fog. He was glad they'd left early. Soon, the coast would be fogged in.

"Lil, Tom, and I were at the beach, not far from the lagoon."

"When was this?"

"Labor Day weekend, 1991."

Lil had bought the cabin in Pescadero in the spring of that year, just after she had moved to San Francisco. "Mom, Dad, Tom, and I were staying at the cabin with Lil. She made sandwiches and a thermos of lemonade. Tom and I went with her to the beach." Brownies, too, he remembered now. After lunch, they'd walked down the beach toward the lagoon. "We were about halfway there when we saw it hopping up and down, struggling to fly." As they approached it, the bird thrashed and squawked, throwing itself from side to side, its legs tangled in fishing line.

Lil had pulled a towel and her Swiss army knife out of her backpack. She handed Tom the knife, and threw the towel over the bird's head, beak, and wings.

"How big?" Ellie asked.

"Maybe 40 inches, wing tip to wing tip. But it didn't weigh much more than ten pounds. Still, it was plenty strong. And very scared."

Lil had sat on the sand, arms around the bird, holding on until, exhausted, it stopped struggling. Tom cut the fishing line. Ben helped remove it. As soon as they cleared the line away, Lil lifted off the towel, the pelican shook itself hard and waddled around, unsteady, as if dazed, uncertain its ordeal was over.

"And then it took off. Just like that."

"What do you think would have happened to it if you hadn't found it?" Ellie asked.

Ben looked at her. "Unless someone else freed it, it would have died. I like to think that it lived to a ripe old age."

Ellie smiled. "A legend in its time."

o o o

By the time they reached the turnoff at Pescadero Beach, the fog had settled in. Five miles inland, where the late afternoon sun touched down on the peaks and slopes of the foothills, Ben turned right at the mailbox at the end of the dirt lane leading to Lil's cabin. Lil had let him pick the color and help her paint it. Once turquoise, it had faded to a pale, silvered grey. *Like the fog,* Ben thought. He downshifted, guiding the Chevy in and out of ruts left by Lil's Jeep.

On both sides of the lane, blossom-studded canes of wild blackberries, *rubus ursinus,* bobbed in the breeze, tapping the sides of the car. Ellie rolled down her window, took a deep breath, and licked her lips. "Warm honey, maybe some lemon—something citrusy, anyway—nutmeg too." She closed her eyes. "Creek, moss, and redwood, with a hint of fog."

Ben imagined high tide, the surf breaking over the sandbar five miles west, the fog rolling on, inland, toward them, gathering fragrances along the way. "The nose knows. Maybe you've missed your calling."

"We could figure out how to distill and bottle it. Call it 'Eau de Pescadero'?" Both laughed.

Ben parked next to the plank bridge across the creek from the cabin, its redwood shingles silvered with age. Five stripling redwoods stood behind it, ferns and trilliums clustered around them.

Ellie got out and stretched. "We could also put in real plumbing. And insulation."

Ben poked his head around the open trunk. "And never leave?"

"That's the idea."

They would graduate from UCSC in six weeks. At the end of the summer, Ellie would leave to spend two years in the Peace Corps, somewhere in Africa. Ben would enter Harvard's graduate program in botany. And then? By mutual agreement, they'd tabled that question.

Ben came around the car, duffel in his left hand, his guitar strap looped over his left shoulder, two bags of groceries cradled in his right arm.

Ellie covered the flat of strawberries with an empty shopping bag, placed the honey, lettuce, and beets on top, lifted the flat out of the backseat and carried it across the footbridge to the cabin. They had stopped at the farm on the outskirts of Davenport. It had an honor system: you took what you wanted from their stand and left money in the cash box under a bushel basket loaded with paper bags bearing a hand-lettered sign that read, "We pick; you pay."

"I could eat all these strawberries and a bushel of blackberries about now," Ellie said.

"Deal." Ben laughed. "Just as long as I don't have to pick the blackberries. It'll be weeks before the blackberries fruit, anyway. We'll be long gone." He took the key from under the watering can on the second step and opened the door.

Lil's security system was a family joke. Matt had cautioned her about her liability. She had laughed. Nothing here worth stealing. No worries.

o o o

In the middle of the room that served as living and dining room, four mismatched ladder-back chairs sat around the old pine table, four friends enjoying a gabfest. Two wicker armchairs, their blue corduroy cushions faded with time and use, sat in front of the woodstove. A queen-sized bed, a dresser, and a cedar blanket chest stood in the alcove along the far wall. To the right were the bathroom and the kitchen.

Until recently, the storage cupboard between the bathroom and kitchen had held boxes of Ben's notes and drawings, as well as Coleman lanterns, flashlights, gardening tools, and extra folding chairs— "For visitors," Lil liked to say. She always paused a beat for the punchline: her nearest neighbors were five miles away, down the main road and most of her family members lived on the East Coast. As far as Ben knew, Lil's friend Billy, a transplanted Texan and a taxi driver, was the only person who visited the cabin regularly. "Not a boyfriend," Lil had insisted. "Just good company. Besides, he likes to drive the Jeep."

The shelf that ran across the wall above the bed held Lil's collection of sea glass and beach pebbles: agate, carnelian, jasper, and quartz. Originally embedded in the sandstone cliffs that lined the coast, freed by erosion, smoothed by the surf, they'd been recycled and scattered on the beach. In this respect, the pebbles Lil had collected resembled her ideas, she said, each one examined, sifted, shaped, and arranged here, in an order that pleased her. "I always have the last word," she had told Ben.

A coffee mug holding a wispy, dried-out bunch of wildflowers sat on top of a note on the table. "Check traps as soon as you arrive, please!" A frowny face followed Lil's signature.

Ben wrinkled his nose. "I'll do it."

"Cheer up," Ellie teased. "If he keeps at it, Sam will clear the place eventually." Sam, Lil's six-month-old poodle, had proved to be a ruthless mouser, cornering and catching his prey, dropping each squirming trophy at Lil's feet. The traps she put out were a symbolic gesture, at best.

Ellie took out the two Hudson's Bay blankets from the chest and spread them over the bed. Ben brought in a bushel of wood and drew a deep breath. "Cedar's the cabin's signature scent, wouldn't you say?"

"And wood smoke."

"Cedar, wood smoke, and damp—lots better than cedar, wood smoke, and dead mice." Ben held up a plastic bag containing the empty mousetraps. "Lil will be pleased."

Lil usually came down from San Francisco one weekend a month. Especially when she'd finished researching a project and was ready to write, she spent her time hiking the trails in the forest and along the creek, or reading her source material, and reviewing her notes—putting them together, taking them apart, until she found her way. "The trees help me think," she told Ellie and Ben the last time they were there together. "The creek helps me sleep. Everything here is in balance and so am I."

His sophomore year at UCSC, Ben had worked out the idea for

his senior project based on the cabin and its surroundings: "Understory: A Forest Floor in Transition." He had handed in his thesis at the beginning of May.

"I'm like Lil. I like to tell stories," he told Ellie. "I suppose you could say my thesis began the day the blackberries caught me, and Lil saved me. How it got here, and the story of the forest's rebirth, must be told."

"Remembered, you mean," Ellie said.

"Who knows what will be left in a hundred—or a thousand—years?"

"Do you think we'll make any difference, that the choices we've made will matter?"

"I'm going to save the forest; you're going to save humanity. Of course, we'll make a difference."

"You'll be at Harvard in your lab. Or collecting samples up in the Harvard Forest. I'll be in Africa, Burkina Faso, or Sudan. It's a big world to save."

"Well, this is where it all began, don't forget. We'll be riding the ripples for years to come." He hugged her.

He plugged Lil's Bluetooth speakers into his phone and switched on KDFC, the San Francisco classical station they liked. While he washed the vegetables and the strawberries, Ellie made polenta. By the time they'd finished their dinner, the fire in the woodstove had banished the damp.

o o o

Drying the dishes after dinner, Ellie looked out at the apron of pale light lapping at the forest's darkness. Sheltered by second-growth redwoods on the creek, the cabin drew in on itself at night, holding them close. She'd been afraid of the dark in the old farmhouse where her family had lived until she was six, waking to the scrabbling of the rats in the attic above her room. Convinced they would find her if they heard her, she lay rigid in her bed, her sheet drawn up over her head until she was gasping for breath. Here, she recognized the night noises—the owl, the fox, the coyote—and enjoyed them. These creatures had their own patterns and were all going about their lives, business as usual.

What animal sounds would she hear in Africa? Wild dogs probably barked and howled there, like coyotes. She wasn't sure about cheetahs. She wouldn't know until the end of the summer, before she left for Africa, if she'd be posted anywhere near places where she'd likely hear any of these animals.

Distracted, she dropped a glass, which shattered at her feet.

Ben, who had been picking out a tune on his guitar, jumped up. "Don't move. I'll get this."

He found the whisk broom and the dustpan in the cupboard, swept up the shards, and dumped them into the trash can under the sink. Was this an omen? Ellie wondered. She didn't believe in omens, so why did this feel like one?

Ben hugged her. "All this stuff is seconds or thirds," he reassured her. "Lil won't care. Come and sit. I'll teach you that French song you asked about."

They pulled the wicker chairs closer to the woodstove and sat facing one another.

Ben had learned the song at camp, a French round about the morning breeze, joyful and free. "It's the only camp song I remember." He taught her the words and they sang it together, softly.

"I was thinking about Mali," Ellie told him. "About the animals there, about whether I'll get used to hearing them at night. I can imagine them in a zoo. But around the corner?"

"I've been wondering about what it will be like to live in a real city." Ben had found an apartment to share in Boston's South End. "Plenty of new noises—sirens, traffic, bells."

"Bells? What bells?"

"Church bells. They're everywhere in Boston and Cambridge."

Ellie giggled. "I'll write about the wild dogs howling; you can write about the bells ringing."

Ben strummed and sang, "The bells are ringing, for me and my gal . . . Wild dogs are howling, for me and my gal . . ." He put the guitar down. "You are, you know." Ben's roommate, a fan of classic musicals, had coaxed Ben to learn this song for a skit they put on in a class they'd taken on romantic comedies. Ben and Ellie had watched it when they first got together.

"Two years we've known each other. The next two will go just as fast."

"So many bells, so little time?"

"Something like that."

○ ○ ○

In mid-April, when he'd finished writing his thesis, Ben had come up to the cabin alone and cleared out his boxes, books, and the sketches he had tacked to the wall. Ellie missed them. The bare spots, the thumbtack marks, only emphasized their absence. The work he had done here, his thesis and his ideas, Ben would take with him when he left California. And Ellie? What would she take?

"Does the place feel empty to you now?" Ellie asked.

Ben settled his guitar on the cedar chest. "After two years collecting, organizing, and managing the piles, I'm done. Are there loose ends? Sure. Those are questions I'll work on at Harvard. So, clearing my stuff out is like taking a deep breath before the next step." He smiled at her. "Call it relief, or something. I don't feel guilty about being here, doing nothing."

"I returned most of my books to the library on Wednesday," Ellie said. "When I stopped by my advisor's office on the way back to my room, she gave me a copy of her latest article. I'll never be an ethnographer."

"Why?"

"Her article—it's just pages and pages of charts and graphs. Where are the people? I'm glad I decided on the Peace Corps before grad school. It'll give me time to sort out what I really want to do. And where I want to be after Africa."

There. She'd said it.

Ben got up from his chair and pulled her up to him, his arms around her waist. "Like the old song says, 'The future is hard to see, what will be, will be.'"

She leaned into him and tucked her head against his shoulder.

o o o

A "meet cute," Joanna had called it. She worried that Ellie took life too seriously, that she didn't have a sense of humor. And, especially, that she didn't know how to flirt or tease or gossip—or care to learn. Until she met Ben, Ellie had wondered if she would ever meet someone who liked her the way she was.

Sophomore year, the anthropology lecture met on Monday morning. Always, Ellie put her book bag under the seat, out of the way, after removing her notebook. The week before the midterm, as she reached down to slide the notebook into her bag, the girl next to her stood up fast, knocking her off balance. Fifteen minutes later, at the library, she opened her book bag. No notebook.

She panicked. In addition to the midterm, she had a presentation to prepare. All her notes and drafts were in the notebook. After a fruitless search of the lecture hall, she went back to her dorm. The phone message taped to her door read: "Found your notebook. Ben Carlson." Ben Carlson? Someone from class? She called him.

Since they lived at opposite sides of the campus, Ben suggested they meet halfway, at Banana Joe's, the snack bar at Crown College. Run and staffed by students, known for its banana muffins, BJ's always had a pot of apple cider warming on the hot plate. Sometimes, passing by on her way to class, Ellie opened the door, closed her eyes, and took a deep breath. Instantly, she was back home in Montpelier on a midwinter afternoon, doing her homework in the kitchen, where a kettle of cider simmered on the stove.

"I'll be there in half an hour," Ben told her. "Look for the Giants cap."

Ellie had fallen right away for his voice and for the quiet, direct way he explained what he would do without making a joke or flirting. As she started to describe what she looked like, he interrupted, "As long as there aren't two of us wearing a Giants cap, we'll be fine."

That evening, a crowd of protesters working together in small groups had occupied BJ's, spreading stacks of poster board and markers on the tables. A whiteboard stood next to the juice dispenser in the rear with slogans like "Peace! Now!" and "Time's UP!" Everyone seemed to be talking at once.

Ben had taken a table in the far corner, opposite the door. Her notebook lay in front of him between two mugs of hot cider. Ellie spotted him right away.

"Hope you like cider."

"It makes me homesick. And happy," she told him.

"I've been waiting for an excuse to talk to you," he said

"Me?" Ellie laughed.

He had noticed her because she was the only person who never looked up from her notebook, regularly turning each page, scribbling furiously, as the lecturer went through that day's talk.

"When I realized that Lost Notebook Girl and Notable Nellie were the same person, I felt like I'd hit a triple." Ben looked at her, fixing her in a steady gaze, gauging her reaction.

Ellie played it straight. "I took a speedwriting course. It's the best way to keep up when he talks about all the stuff that isn't in the book."

He took this in with a nod.

"How 'bout we trade? Cider at BJ's for a look at your notes."

"Throw in a muffin?"

"Sold to the lady with the notebook."

When Ellie went home for Christmas, Joanna badgered her for details. "He's not just the guy who found your notebook, Ellie."

He wasn't good looking—in a good way. Nerdy, she'd thought. Until he smiled. His smile cleared a space for the two of them, made it seem they were the only people in the room.

He wanted to be a botanist. He was an accomplished artist who produced pen-and-ink drawings of wildflowers and ferns that were precise in every detail. After a few weeks, Ellie realized one more thing that drew her to him: He'd already decided on a major, one that would combine environmental studies and botany. His certainty and his willingness to listen to her talk about her uncertainty gave her the opportunity she needed to consider her own options. Maybe anthropology. Maybe sociology. Maybe some combination, a double major like the one Ben had chosen.

Ben had spent several summers at Camp Overlook on Lake Champlain. Ellie had taken a class trip to tour the Bellevue Avenue mansions in Newport, near Middletown, where Ben's family lived.

"Satisfied?" Ellie grinned. "Our paths have already crossed."

Jo giggled. "On a scale of one to five on the meet-cute meter, this one's a five."

○ ○ ○

They went out to sit on the wooden deck chairs beside the creek, facing upstream. A few stars gleamed faintly through the thickening fog.

Another time, earlier that spring, they had heard the hoot of an owl on the hunt, a sound that echoed back to them across the creek. Tonight, only the creek's ripples and splashes disturbed the stillness. Ben lit the Coleman lantern; Ellie wrapped a wool throw around her shoulders. Here, they could live their lives day by day, undisturbed by thoughts about the future. Even the phone could be turned off. Ellie thought she could be happy stepping back from the pressure to do, to be, to hurry forward. Watching Ben now, leaning back in the chair, legs stretched out, she imagined he could be, too.

"It'll go fast," Ben said, as if picking up a conversation they had interrupted just a moment ago.

"We can always write," Ellie smiled. "We'll figure something out." *We'll always have Pescadero*, she thought.

After learning that mobile internet service was available but unreliable, Ellie had found out about sending air mail from Bamako. "They use aerograms. Do you know what those are?"

"Sure. When we were kids, Lil sent us aerograms when she went to Europe. Not sure I can find them here, anymore. But airmail? Sure."

Ellie imagined the letters they would exchange, their thoughts condensed into pictograms or symbols each of them would decipher, coaxing from them how an experience felt and looked, reading between the lines. "Let's say I write one aerogram a week and mail them on my day off from Bamako. They could take a week or ten days to get to Boston."

"I can't wait," Ben said, smiling. "If I'm lucky, I'll get all four—or five—on the same day. It'll be like reading a novel. Anyway, I'm going to keep a journal, too. You'll be able to read it when you get back."

Ellie made a face. "I don't plan to keep a journal."

"A list, then," Ben said. "Just jot down what you don't tell everyone else." His eyes, intent on hers, gleamed in the lantern light.

"My secrets, you mean?" She laughed. "Do you write yours in your journal?"

"Not everything. Some things I keep to myself."

"Like what?"

"Things I don't understand."

"Could you give me a 'for instance'?"

Ben looked away. "Things I've done that embarrassed me, things that have frightened me."

"Tell me one."

Ben cleared his throat. "Once, a friend invited me to come with him and his family to Cape Cod. I told him my parents wouldn't let me."

"You didn't want to go to the Cape?"

"Sure I did. I loved going out there. But his dad was a mean drunk. I was afraid of him."

"And you couldn't tell your friend that."

"No way. I was only eight. I didn't know how to talk about it. His mom talked to my mom, who told her of course I could go if I wanted to. She asked me why I had lied. I couldn't tell her the real reason. Looking back now, as well as being afraid of his father, I was ashamed for the kid. I guess I thought if I told the truth, other people would find out and he'd suffer for it. Anyway, I didn't go. And that was it, the end of our friendship." Ben stretched his arms over his head, leaned back, and looked up into the trees. "His dad died a few years later in a car crash. He'd been drinking." He sat up and turned toward Ellie. "Have you ever done anything like that?"

"I've done things I was ashamed of, things no one but me knows about." Ellie leaned close. "I used to pick up stuff."

"'Pick up' as in 'steal'?"

"Shhhh. Not so loud, or I'll have to kill you." At the sound of their laughter, an animal splashed out of the creek and up the bank into the woods behind the cabin.

"Anything else you'd like to share with the doctor today?"

"I'm thinking."

Ben mimed adjusting spectacles and stood up. "Take your time, my dear. Chamomile or peppermint?"

"Chamomile with a dash of honey, honey."

o o o

Ellie closed her eyes, absorbing the sound of the creek running nearby, imagined lying in the water, feeling it wash over her, cool and clear, carrying away the past, preparing her for the future. The shallow creek carved a narrow winding bed below the cabin, its sandy bottom cradling stones that jostled one another as the water flowed over them.

She had sat one day on the bank, perched on a mossy stone, mesmerized by the current swirling into and out of a pocket. It was moving fast enough to lift and nudge a stone momentarily onto its side. Then, like a hen sinking into a bed of straw, the stone rolled back onto its belly and revealed its back, thickly grown with green, feathery moss.

The simple shift altered nothing. Not immediately. Eventually, though, the movement of the water and the friction of the sand would shape the stone, imprinting their own story on it—grooves where the stone was soft and miniature hillocks where it resisted.

Before she met Ben, accustomed to being on her own, to keeping herself to herself, Ellie had been comfortable as an outsider, content to have acquaintances rather than close friends. It was different now. Her life and Ben's had become intertwined, like the wild cucumber plant vines twining over the woodpile and up into a nearby Douglas fir.

When Ben returned with the tea, she was ready. The current had shifted her, put her down in the same place, only with new feelings—feelings to share with Ben, to understand.

He set the two mugs on the table and handed her the wool throw. She pulled it around her shoulders and sipped her tea.

The owl hooted again. Ben leaned forward, looking down the creek. "It's moved downstream. Maybe it's tracking a skunk. Lil thinks it's a great horned owl." He leaned into the silence, waiting for Ellie to begin.

o o o

After Ellie finished first grade, her mother decided to move with her and her two sisters, Eve and Joanna, down the mountain where they were living into Montpelier, five miles away. No more snowbound winters in the farmhouse. No more getting stuck on the road in mud season. Ellie was six. She had friends in town. She was ready to move closer to them and to school.

Their father had refused even to consider the idea. So, her mother packed the three of them into the Jeep and moved in with a friend. It took her less than a week to find a house within walking distance of their school and a short drive—on paved, plowed streets—to the grocery store. Her ultimatum brought their father around. He soon joined them in town. But the move didn't resolve his business troubles.

A dedicated, compassionate veterinarian, he collected IOUs for his services, which he stowed in a box under a table in the back of his clinic, a room off the garage. No call went unanswered. He listened, commiserated, and waved away the embarrassment and the excuses, telling his clients, "You can pay me next time." Ellie's mother became adept at juggling the bills, leaving her own trail of IOUs, trusting his assurances that circumstances would improve soon.

There were no second helpings. Ellie wore hand-me-downs, all provided by the older daughters of one of her mother's friends. She and her sisters each got one toy or book for Christmas and their birthdays. They shared everything. Even their bathwater.

She, Joanna, and Eve liked playing dress-up and putting on plays with other kids in the neighborhood, plays based on stories they made up or ones they knew. Teetering in high heels, decked out in their mother's old dresses and their grandmother's cast-off costume jewelry, they took turns playing queens, princesses, fairy godmothers, sorcerers, and witches.

Star of every show, Ellie also directed. To keep her two sisters in line, she let them choose their own costumes. Until their father brought home the TV—a client had paid him in cash, for a change—wishes-come-true stories were their only escape from their parents' discord.

When Ellie was seven, a black-and-white portrait of Marilyn Monroe appeared on the wall behind the candy counter at the neighborhood mom-and-pop store among the other black-and-white photos of stars the owner of the shop had collected. Her black-gloved left hand propped under her chin, her eyes half-shut, leaning toward the viewer, Marilyn smiled at the world. The first time she saw the photo, Ellie stared at Marilyn's mouth—her full lips gleaming, her teeth slightly parted, as if she were about to taste something delicious, something forbidden. After that, Ellie made excuses to go to the store. At night, in the dark, lying in her bed, she closed her eyes and Marilyn appeared, smiling down at her.

Ellie couldn't stop thinking about Marilyn's mouth. Red lipstick. It had to be. Otherwise, what was the point? She was practicing the smile one day, looking into the bathroom mirror, when Jo barged in.

"Ick! What's wrong with you? You look sick."

Some nights Ellie watched the headlights slide across the ceiling and down the wall into the far corner of her room. She waited until everyone was in bed to sneak into the bathroom and look for Marilyn's smile. Some nights she didn't go to sleep until dawn, absorbed for hours in running her forefinger over her lips and imagining she was applying lipstick, that she was Marilyn.

Walking home from school, she passed a Walgreen's on Main Street. Sometimes she wandered the aisles to savor the aroma, a mix of cologne and the vanilla odor of cellophane and plastic.

One drizzly winter day, she went into the store. It was so dark outside, the overhead lights seemed to strike sparks off every surface. The back of her neck prickled, a feeling that didn't stop until she reached the lipstick display. Six rows of lipstick tubes lined up, each with a plastic color chip and label below it. The first row, which sat at Ellie's eye level, held twenty tubes, each a different shade of red. Which one would Marilyn choose, she wondered?

She had to hurry, before another shopper or a salesgirl discovered her and asked what she was doing there. Tube by tube, Ellie examined the chips: "True Red," "Simply Red," on and on. Then "Red as Red," the last one in the row. Why that one? She just had a feeling. Even if it wasn't Marilyn's color, its name made it sound like it should be. She slipped the tube out of the rack and slid it into her pocket.

She looked around. The aisle was empty. She looked up. Above her, a vision of Marilyn's face floated under the lights. She smiled at Ellie, lips parted, teeth glistening.

After dinner that night and every night that week, instead of watching TV with Jo and Eve, Ellie went to the room they shared, closed the door, and wedged a footstool against it. She reached under her mattress, where she had hidden it, and pulled out the tube of lipstick. Lying in the dark, she removed the cap slowly, and inhaled. After a few weeks, the fragrance faded. In the shop, Marilyn's smile dulled.

She could have dropped the tube into a storm drain or thrown it into the trash bin in the lavatory at school. Instead, she put it in a box under her sweaters in her bottom drawer, together with the lace-edged handkerchief her grandmother had given her, the silver dollar she'd received for her sixth birthday, and the daisy-shaped button she'd found on the playground.

Wandering the aisles of Walgreen's one day, she found a sewing kit—thimbles, spools of thread, needles and straight pins, a pin cushion in the shape of a tomato. Ellie had watched her grandmother hem a skirt for her, holding the sewing needle in her right hand, the thimble on the tip of her left index finger, moving the needle through the fabric, stitch by stitch, until it touched the thimble with a soft click.

Ellie had tried on the thimble, smooth and cool to the touch. She'd had it since she was Ellie's age, her grandmother said, laughing. "Fifty years, Ellie, imagine that!"

Ellie turned her back to the kit on the shelf, as if searching for something across the aisle. Checking to see no one was watching her, she reached behind her, lifted the sewing kit off the display shelf and slid it into the deep pocket of her winter coat. At home, she placed the sewing kit in the box with the lipstick, the silver dollar, and the button.

As she added to her collection, she examined each object, reliving the thrill of discovery, her fear of being caught. Each one belonged to her in ways nothing else did. Only she knew of their existence. Whenever she was tired, scared, or bored, she closed her eyes and imagined the box, imagined opening it, removing the contents, feeling the shape, size, and texture of each object. The memories they inspired, the story they helped her tell herself were all that was certain during very uncertain times.

She buried the box in the woods behind her grandparents' house the day after she graduated from high school. "It was time. Like now," she told Ben.

"An ending and a beginning?"

"That's what it feels like."

"You never used the lipstick?"

"By the time I was old enough, I'd figured out I'm not the lipstick type."

"You mean, not the Marilyn Monroe type?"

Ellie laughed. "In the eighth grade when all the other girls were wearing padded bras, stockings, and learning how to walk in high heels, I figured out I was most definitely not a glamour puss. Too much trouble. All that posing. And lipstick?" She rubbed her arms hard, as if she'd felt a draft. "The minute you smile or talk, it begins to wear off."

"Once I kissed a girl who was wearing lipstick. I could taste the perfume. Never again."

Ben stood and stretched. He reached for Ellie's hand and pulled her up.

"What about your stories, your end of bargain?" she asked.

"Tomorrow. Just like this."

She kissed him. "Deal."

o o o

The sound of water dripping on the roof woke Ellie. They had fallen asleep spooning. She felt Ben against her, and pressed closer to him, gently.

"Yes?" he whispered.

She reached for his hand on her stomach, threaded her fingers between his.

He lifted her hair and kissed the back of her neck.

o o o

The next evening after dinner, they turned out all the lights except the one on the side table between the armchairs. Ben opened the door of the woodstove. For a while they sat, watching the embers flicker then fade.

A wind had come up. A branch clattered against the side of the cabin; a shower of needles spattered the roof. In a few weeks, Ellie would be in Berkeley, taking an intensive French course; Ben would be back in Newport, where he had a summer job working as a gardener for the Preservation Society, before starting his first term at Harvard.

Ben took an eight-by-twelve-inch envelope from the drawer in the side table and handed it to Ellie. She opened it and removed a matted pen-and-ink drawing of a wild Bleeding Heart in bloom, its heart-shaped flowers dangling from single stems among fringed leaves. It was one of dozens of drawings Ben had done over the last two years—one she particularly liked.

"I wanted you to have something to take with you from here, something light, flat, and packable."

Ellie held it to her nose. "It even smells like the cabin."

"You know that old idea about how if you leave something behind in a place you care about, it means you'll be back?" He reached for her hand. "I believe if you carry a piece of a place you love with you, it guarantees you'll come back."

"It still doesn't seem real that we're about to pack up and leave all this." Ellie closed her eyes. When she opened them, Ben was staring into space, frowning. "There are so many memories here, for you especially."

"Ever since I turned my thesis in, I've been having flashbacks. As if I'm clearing the deck. Putting away childish things." He made air quotes. "Like you, burying your keepsake box. It's a kind of preparation, I guess. I don't really know who I am. Yet. Maybe the flashbacks are clues. I study how plants grow, observe the process. I know that process. I understand the cycle. It shouldn't be that different for people, should it?"

"Isn't that because we can't stand outside ourselves, observe ourselves, the way we can observe a growing plant?"

"Yes, but even if I could do that, I wouldn't be observing the whole picture, because I need to feel what's in here," Ben touched his head, then his heart, "as well as see what's out there, what I do, my actions." He pointed at the drawing, gestured at the forest outside. "Sometimes I think that what I think and feel, and what I do, are as mysterious to me as they would be to any stranger." He shook his head. "Especially the memories."

Ellie leaned toward him, reeling him in. "Your turn, your secret."

"My turn." His face stilled.

Ben slid down in the chair, legs outstretched, ankles crossed. "I told you part of this story the first time we came here, about that time I got stuck under the blackberries."

Of course, Ellie had wanted to see the exact spot. On her hands and knees in the lane, peering under the dense, towering bushes, she had looked up at him, wide-eyed. She couldn't imagine crawling under there, she told him, never mind being caught in the tangle of shoots and canes, thick with prickles.

"Tell me the rest."

His mother decided to make blackberry pies. She had sent them out to the lane to pick the berries while she prepared pie crusts. Although it was the end of the season, she was certain they would bring back more than enough fruit for two pies.

"I could see berries on the ground under the bushes so when I found that opening, one some animal had made, a fox maybe, to get down to the creek, I crawled in."

Laughing and talking as they picked, Lil, Tom, and his dad moved up the lane toward the cabin. It was dark and cool under the bushes, the soil tangy with dust, rotting berries, and something else—something wild. Shafts of sunlight penetrated here and there, leading him deeper under the thicket in his search. On his belly, elbowing his way along, he soon filled his basket. The sound of the others was fainter now. Careful not to upset his basket, he drew his knees to his chest and turned around. The opening to the lane had disappeared.

Pushing the basket of berries ahead of him, he inched his way back, thinking he would spot the opening when he got closer to it. When a cane snagged his sock, he yanked it; it snagged his shoe and uprooted another cane, which latched onto his shorts and dug into his thigh. He yanked again. Beside him, another cane grabbed and hooked his collar. Shoe, shorts, shirt. He couldn't move.

"That's when I heard the sound, a grunting sound nearby. I couldn't turn around or look around to see. I closed my eyes, listening hard, holding my breath. The noise stopped. I exhaled. The sound started up again."

"What was it? What was making the noise?" Ellie asked.

"It was me. It was coming from me."

"What happened then?"

"I blacked out."

When he came to, he saw Lil crouched in the lane, peering under the bushes. He said her name. She moved away. He shouted then and she heard him. As soon as she saw him, she lay down in the lane and reached in. Their fingers touched. She told him to lie still, to count from one to sixty. She would be back soon with her loppers. Tom and his dad came and counted with him until Lil returned. As she cut away the canes, his dad pulled them out and piled them on the other side of the lane. Free at last, Ben crawled out with his basket of berries.

"How long did it take to cut away the canes?"

"Maybe ten minutes. But it seemed like hours."

"What happened then?"

"Everyone started talking at once, you know, asking me why I'd crawled in there in the first place."

"Well, it makes sense to me, why you did."

"Yeah, but I couldn't tell them. I was scared."

"Scared of what?"

"I'd blacked out and I was ashamed, I guess."

"I don't understand."

"It's just, you know, I shouldn't have been scared. Shouldn't have blacked out."

"So you never told anyone about the blackout?"

"Just you," Ben said.

"You had a panic attack. That's nothing to be ashamed of."

"Maybe not. But I was."

"Have you had any blackouts since then?"

"Only once. The time Tom capsized on the lake when I ran back to camp to get help." He sat up and reached for Ellie's hand. "No one else knows about that one either."

Lil taught him about the blackberry, *rubus ursinus*. In the shady, wet areas along the creek, huckleberries had flourished. They were West Coast natives, like the blackberries. But over the years, as loggers cleared out the redwoods and firs up and down the creek, sun-loving plants like blackberries had moved in, helped along by the birds and other animals.

He had imagined the birds, squirrels, and chipmunks eating the berries and excreting the seeds. That would be worth studying, he thought now. He'd call it "Excreta and Species Preservation in California's Coastal Woodlands."

"I remember how the blackberries got here," Ellie interrupted. "I even remember the name."

Rubus ursinus. Bramble Bear. A relative of the loganberry and the boysenberry. Ben reflected again on the family relationship—the prickly blackberry, the thornless loganberry—and about being six years old and caught in the bramble bear's clutches, about his panic attack.

He had sat in the pool under the waterfall to wash away the prickles. When he was dry, after Lil slathered him with antiseptic, she showed him drawings of the plant, the first botanical drawings he had ever seen.

As his mother predicted, they had brought back plenty of berries for her pies. But not even the baked berries' intense, caramelized sweetness could make up for the gritty seeds, which got stuck in his teeth.

Sitting beside him at the pine table after dinner, her shirt sleeves rolled up to her elbows, Lil talked about *rubus ursinus*, about its stems, leaves, flowers, and berries. Ben looked up into her face—her blue eyes dark and focused, her attention absorbed by the illustration. It was his first glimpse of what it meant to be in sync, in time and space, with a process and a commitment. Now, if someone asks how he became interested in botany he tells the story, describes his sense of wholeness expressed now, years later, in his study of plants and their myriad relationships to each other and to their habitat.

Lil helped him trace the illustration, leaf by leaf, stem by stem, until his finished drawing matched the original. She encouraged him to apply to UCSC. She'd made the Pescadero cabin her refuge. For Ben, it had become both refuge and workspace.

Ellie smoothed the throw over her lap. They didn't speak again for a while. Except for the faint sound of water dripping on the roof from the redwoods, the forest was silent.

o o o

The next morning, they got up early and hiked up the creek to the pool where they'd once seen a steelhead. The ferns along the trail dripped steadily.

Ellie crouched at the edge of the pool, reached into the water, and pulled out a small oval stone, about the size of a domino, pale brown with bands of darker brown running through it. "It looks like one of Lil's beach pebbles," she said. "An agate, I think." She had taken a course about the California Gold Rush with a mineralogist who had shared his passion for what he called "mining's dust mice" on hikes in San Mateo's mining country. Ellie grinned.

"Remind me."

"Harmony, trust, and stability. And confidence and strength. The power of agate." Ellie looked down into the creek. "Also, it'll help you keep your promises."

"Says who?"

"Lil. And the guy who taught the Gold Rush course."

She rubbed the stone dry on her jeans and offered it to Ben. "I will keep a journal."

Ben held Ellie's hand, pressing her right palm onto the agate in his hand. "Me too."

Lil
2010

Pale green walls, a Danish modern desk and armchairs, photographs of tree ferns—the office reminded me of the French spa I'd written about for Travel and Leisure. *And petite, ash-blond Amy Whitlock—Dr. Whitlock—reminded me of Joelle, my best friend in high school. She was a problem-solver, too.*

Amy hugs me. She always does. Was there anything different in the way she hugged me today? A clue? I can't tell. The pleasantries we exchange are barely audible over my pounding heart. Seated beside me, she opens my folder and smooths it flat on her lap.

"It's cancer, Lil." Her gaze holding mine, she takes my hand. "First, a lumpectomy. Depending on what we find—the margins, the lymph nodes—followed by a course of radiation and, possibly, chemo."

I imagine a battery of cannons, locked, loaded, and aimed at my left breast. "This is after," I think. "After begins now."

By the time she finishes explaining the surgery and the treatment plan—my treatment plan, she called it—I am convinced: together, we will slay the dragon.

o o o

Two years later, a year from the day I'd learned I was in remission, I heard Amy describe the results of the tests. In my mind's eye, I watched a seesaw: "remission" sat on one side, "recurrence" on the other. Tipping one way, then the other, the two sides seemed evenly matched. Which one would prevail, I wondered?

"It's back," Amy said. "I am so sorry." Amy can manage the disease, ease my symptoms. And she always holds out hope: There are clinical trials, she reminds me, and one of the drugs they're testing now may help.

For the time being, at least I'm maintaining.

One day at a time.

o o o

Every day used to be linked to a yesterday, holding its own, connecting the past to the future, like the paragraphs linked, polished, weighed, and measured for one of my articles. Now, each day, each present moment, glitters like fool's gold. I watch the shadows play across my living room floor, inhale the fragrance of lavender and rose geranium wafting in from the garden. Every detail, from the dance of the dust motes in the sunlight to the spider bobbing in her web in the corner of my office, mocks my illusions. Yes, tomorrow will come, but where will I be then?

As a travel writer, I've always observed the "no-bigger-than-a-breadbox" principle—hand luggage, only, portable souvenirs. The handmade ceramic tiles I've brought home are tangible proof of another time and place where, for a day or two, I stepped out of myself, settled in, and lived as a native might. Holding one of them, watching how the colors change in the light, revives the feeling of the sun on my skin, the way the shadows of the plane tree fell across the café table the day I visited the ceramics shop, the sights and sounds of the villages I passed through in pursuit of yet another anecdote to share with my readers, something that might conjure for them what it was like to inhabit a different world, if only for a moment, if only vicariously.

Surrounded by the pieces I've collected, their colors and shapes vivid against my cottage's white walls, I can recall where and when

I found each one—my conversations with the artisans, their stories seamlessly linked, one to the other, finite, clear, precious. When I leave, I'll take the stories and my memories with me. The objects will remain behind, like shells washed up and abandoned on the beach.

Sam, my standard poodle, is the exception.

Eight years ago, I spent three weeks in Béziers, France, researching an article about Languedoc-Roussillon vintners for *Gourmet Magazine*. One morning, as I was leaving the hotel to drive to a winery in Le Somail, the *patronne* stopped me at the door, dabbing at her eyes with the hem of her apron.

"Madame, please? Please come."

I followed her through the hotel lobby and out to the courtyard off the kitchen, where a covered wicker basket sat on a bench next to the trash bins.

"Please, madame." She gestured at the basket. "A dog, a little dog." She shook her head. "My son found him this morning under the bin." She sobbed. "We don't know what to do with him."

The moment I lifted the lid and picked him up, I stammered out questions like a first-year French student. A ball of apricot fluff, the puppy wagged and wiggled, licked my chin and my ears. Love at first sight for me. For him, too.

As far as I could tell, he was in fine shape. Not an emergency, then. At least, not exactly. He was healthy, but he was a foundling; he needed a home. How did the manager know I'd fall for him? Just doing Fate's bidding, I told myself later.

As I negotiated the arcana of inoculations and certifications, and the restrictions on exporting (and traveling with) a puppy, second thoughts nearly undid the deal. Realistically, how was I going to keep a puppy with me in my studio in San Francisco? I was away on assignment nearly four months a year. Who would take care of him then? By the time I had sorted out the travel details, I'd decided to leave the future in Fate's hands. Hadn't she brought us together? Sam was mine, as I was his. For the first time in my life, I checked my carry-on so he could travel in a carrier under my seat. It was a non-stop flight, Paris to San Francisco. He slept the whole way.

Finding Sam, taking him back with me, made me realize that the fizz had gone out of my wanderlust. My willingness to go anywhere, do (almost) anything for a good story on the spur of the moment, was sputtering. For Sam's sake, as much as my own, I needed to look for a real home.

I took three months off to house-hunt and to help Sam adjust to living in a city. When a friend decided to sell his cottage on Napier Lane on Telegraph Hill, I bought it. Fate, again. Built in 1910, the nine-hundred-square-foot, two-story cottage needed more than a scrub-down. A contractor gutted it, combined the two upstairs rooms into an office and reconfigured the four rooms downstairs into a living room/kitchen, two bedrooms, and bathroom.

I learned about mortgage rates, property tax, and homeowner's insurance, which replaced rising air fares and foreign exchange rates in conversations with friends. Dog training manuals and weekly classes with Sam gave me a reason to reconnect with the city, to walk it daily, as I had done when I first moved to the Bay area.

On the day I filled my Jeep with the last carton of books, I discovered how much Sam had learned. "Sit," I said. Sam sat still while I attached his leash. "Let's go." He walked with me out the door and stayed beside me, taking the stairs at my pace. He sat, unprompted, while I opened the door. As soon as he saw the Jeep, he pranced in place without tugging at the leash or pawing at me.

"Good boy," I told him. He looked up at me. Of course.

o o o

Thanks to the pale oak floors and white-washed walls, new windows and extended verandah, the cottage is airy and open. Maybe because I've lived in hotel rooms for so long, it also feels elegant and spacious, like a suite at the Grand Hotel de la Minerve in Rome.

From my desk upstairs, I look out through the trees at Grace Marchant's terraced garden and the Filbert Steps, the Berkeley hills, and the Bay Bridge. Occasionally, a cherry-headed conure, one of Telegraph Hill's wild parrots, perches on my windowsill, clucking softly, sharing the latest gossip.

I'd be lost in a house like the Victorian Grace and I grew up in in Connecticut, with its twelve-foot ceilings and dark corners. Grace's house in Middletown, Rhode Island, a former sea captain's home, resembles our childhood home enough to be its fraternal twin. The difference? Mainly, the clutter and energy of the three children who live there.

The first time Grace visited me, when I showed her my studio on Market Street, she pointed out it was the same size as her bathroom. Her rambling Stick Victorian, with its views across Easton's Beach to Newport's Cliff Walk, suits Grace and Matt; there's plenty of room for them and the three kids. They can be together as much or as little as they like.

When I visit, I stay in the guest room, a bedroom and adjoining bath. But the house feels like an oversized coat whose sleeves drape awkwardly over your hands, no matter how you roll them up, a garment you long to throw off the minute you put it on. If it weren't for the surrounding farmland and woods, and the beach at the foot of the hill, I wouldn't stay more than a week. As it is, when the kids were young and I visited for two weeks occasionally in the summer, I spent most of my time outdoors with them.

o o o

When I moved into the cottage, I had assignments lined up that would keep me away for several weeks at a time for the next year. I couldn't leave Sam alone, and I didn't want to board him. A neighbor told me about Billy, a cab driver who moonlights as a house- and pet-sitter.

When Billy appeared at my door, on time for our first appointment, Sam greeted him like an old friend, head-butting him and offering him play-bows until Billy sat on the floor and took him in his lap.

About six feet three in his boots, Billy had to duck to come in the front door. He carried a Stetson hat and wore a denim shirt with pearl snap buttons and a bolo tie with a silver and turquoise slide. He looked like an extra from a Hollywood Western. His face had that kind of rugged look until you reached his eyes—blue, welcoming, guileless.

At first, I had to ask him to repeat himself.

"West Texas, ma'am," he said, "where the real cowboys come from. You'll get used to it, I reckon. The drawl, I mean."

I didn't argue the point.

He accepted a cup of tea and told me his story. "I'm a city boy, born and bred," he began, with no trace of a drawl.

"So the drawl is—"

"What everyone expects. I realized right away that anyone you meet in this city jumps to the same conclusion: if you're from Texas, you must be a cowboy."

"Just like if you say you're from the East Coast, people assume you're a New Yorker?"

He laughed. "Like that."

"Tell me the story."

"I was born in Austin. Lived there until I went to UCLA, on a swimming scholarship. LA?" He shook his head. "Too many cars, too much smog, too full of people on the make, too full of itself."

"When did you graduate?" Billy's face showed wear and tear, the kind that shows up on all of us in middle age, but I couldn't tell into which end of middle age he fell.

"I dropped out after my sophomore year, went back to Texas, and got a job on a ranch."

"So you were a cowboy?"

"I sure tried to be." He chuckled and sipped his tea. "I had a good time riding with the real cowboys, driving the cattle, but I was much better at fixing and tinkering. I put motors back together; repaired water pumps; invented a doohickey for raising and lowering the branding pen gates." He gave me a searching look.

"I'm not bored," I said.

He shrugged. "After twenty years, I got tired. Decided to come to San Francisco for a while. I'd always wanted to see that bridge." He grinned.

"What bridge?"

It's a lame joke, but he laughed.

"So now you're driving a cab."

"I'm a forty-eight-year-old ex-cowboy, ma'am. I've been driving my cab for nearly ten years."

I decided then and there, Billy, Sam, and I—and the cottage—would get along fine. Fate, it seemed, had again tipped the scale in my favor.

I called Dana to tell her I'd solved my what-to-do-with-Sam problem.

"Driving a cab around San Francisco can't be easy," she said. "Sounds like a grind, really."

"No harder than driving cattle, Billy says, although the traffic is just as ornery. Where it beats ranching is in the shoveling-poop department."

"So, he house-sits and pet-sits, too?"

"Mostly as a favor for friends, it turns out. Lucky for me, we have a friend in common."

"Will he take care of Sam and the cottage for free?"

"No way. I told him if he won't accept payment, I'll keep looking."

Dana laughed. "You sound like Mom in management mode."

"It worked. He agreed. He always takes time off in February to ski. He'll put the money I pay him into his vacation fund."

o o o

Billy arranged his schedule, so Sam was never alone for more than five hours. Sometimes when I was home, he stopped by for coffee. Often, instead of a pastry from Café Trieste, he delivered stories of his life as cab driver. "I should write an article," I told him. "Every time I take a cab, the cabby tells me stories."

Billy chuckled. "*A Thousand-and-One Cab Rides?*"

He drove me to my appointment the day I learned my diagnosis and took charge of Sam on days I was too sick from the radiation and, later, the chemo to walk him. Sam and I would have been lost without him.

o o o

I spend the mornings revising an article about Portugal's Alentejo wine region for *Travel & Leisure*—checking references, spellings, and phone numbers of the hotels and restaurants I visited, selecting photos—and waiting for Amy's daily check-in call. Snoring softly, Sam lies in his bed beside my desk, occasionally opening an eye to check on me.

There is no longer a scintilla of hope I will be cured, but I cannot stifle the surge of optimism. A new drug. A combination of existing drugs. Something will turn up. If you've had cancer, you know the rules: Recurrence is the flip side of remission. When hope of remission dies, hope for more, new, better treatment rises—not a cure, but rather comfort care, a respite, a few more precious months of the life you will no longer take for granted.

The phone rings.

"Let me go over the results," Amy says, her tone calm, matter-of-fact. "Then we'll talk about what we're going to do." Straightforward as usual, Amy continues. Eyes closed, I listen, imagining a dial, tracking the needle. The needle on the dial passes "now," and "results from a clinical trial." It stops between "metastasis" and "comfort care." Somewhere, a door slams.

The golds, greens, reds, and blues of the ceramic tiles hanging on the whitewashed walls around me gleam in the sunlight streaming through the branches and leaves of the fig tree outside my window. My bookshelves hold the guides, memoirs, maps, and boxes of slides I've accumulated over the last twenty years. Propped up on the top shelf, Dana, Tom, and Ben, Grace and Matt, smile down at me from photographs taken on the beach in Newport, at the cabin in Pescadero, so familiar, so far away.

I imagine a cancer cell dividing, the microscopic, inescapable enemy, my present and my future, the wall that's building in me, around me. There's no way out. Not this time.

"I'm so sorry, Lil," The sound of Amy's quiet voice reminds me that she's not just my doctor. She has become a dear friend.

o o o

When I was first diagnosed, Dana took on assignments about research in breast cancer diagnosis, treatments, and recovery. Our roles reversed. I'd offered advice and pointers at the start of her career as a science writer, now she was my guide, helping me ask questions about my therapy and prognosis. She phoned often, sent me Kate Matthews cartoons, listened late at night when I called, too tired and ill to make sense of what was happening.

Noon here; three o'clock in Boston.

She picks up on the first ring. "It's me, Dana."

The sound of traffic on Beacon Street outside Dana's condo overlaps a siren's wail, rising in waves up the Filbert Steps from Sansome to my office, where I sit on the floor, Sam stretched out beside me.

On her end, a chair slides across the floor, papers rustle. "Tell me everything. I'm taking notes."

As if our brain waves synchronize when we most need one another, we often speak in shorthand, our conversations like a fast singles volley, without interruption. I'm especially grateful for this today. The essentials. That's all I can manage. I pick up my teacup. The sip of tea nearly doesn't make it over the dam stuck in my throat.

"There're tumors in my bones. And in my liver." Stage IV, the devious, shapeshifting monster that's eating me alive. "Can you come out for a week?"

"For as long as you'll have me. I'll bring work with me, but let's do something fun, okay?"

"Billy, Sam, and I have a plan for that." We didn't. At least not yet. But the thought of making one made me smile.

A motorcycle accelerates up Beacon Street in Boston. Below my window, in the garden, someone's playing a guitar.

"I'll call you when I know my flight."

There's a 9:30 a.m. non-stop to San Francisco. Maybe she'll be here in time for dinner. Maybe Billy can pick her up.

"Have you talked to Mom?" Her hesitant tone tells me she wants me to do this sooner rather than later.

When I spoke to Grace a month ago, she badgered me. "Get a second opinion, Lil. There must be someone at Stanford you can talk to." The next day, she left a message about a clinic in Mexico, a miracle cure—mushrooms, or something. If I call her, she'll smother me—mother me—in her own worry. And she'll try to manage me. I need time. Time for the news to settle. Time to rally.

"Not yet."

"Maybe while I'm there?"

"Maybe, yes."

o o o

Mama walks in the front door, leaning on the nurse. I get up from the bottom stair, run to her. Mrs. Cullen lifts me, carries me screaming up the stairs to my room. Grace follows us. As soon as Mrs. Cullen sets me down on my bed, she leaves, closing the door behind her. Grace leans against it, arms crossed, eyeing me. That's my earliest memory of Mama. I was four.

Each time she came home, I clung to her. Each time she left, I ran after her, crying. She was sick, Grace said. But I didn't learn what was wrong with her until after she died. I guessed it had something to do with me in the way Papa looked at me, as if I were a stranger, in the way Grace's face closed when I asked when Mama would come home again. I was in a dark, empty space, looking for a light, feeling my way around the walls. And then she died. I was eight.

It was Grace who comforted me when Mama was away. Like a shadow or a ghost, Papa drifted in and out. He worked. He came home. He communicated in monosyllables and left Grace no choice. She had to take charge. She fed, dressed, bathed, and entertained me. And I submitted until I became strong enough to resist.

The more she told me what to do, the more I did the opposite. I answered her Peter Pan collar blouses, knee-length kilts, and bobby socks with tie-dyed shirts, miniskirts, and tights. I died my hair black; learned how to use a kohl pencil to blacken my eyebrows, line my lids. I became determined to find my own way, regardless of the consequences. Of course, we were opposites. I took advantage and she bore the brunt. Only when Grace had her own children did I consider the toll Mama's death had taken, that taking charge of me was a role forced on her, that she had no choice.

However opposite we were in most ways, Grace and I shared an abiding grief and anger at Mama's death, grief and anger rooted in and nurtured by a deep well of self-blame. In Grace's case, it was, "If only I hadn't talked back that time, if only I'd paid more attention." In my case, it was, "If only I hadn't been born."

I'm forty-eight; Grace is fifty-three. Like Tom and Ben, Grace and I could not be more different in the choices we've made, the lives we've lived. But Dana and I are close, in our life's work and in our emotional compatibility. We've become best friends.

o o o

While Dana was an undergraduate at Boston College, I booked flights as often as I could through Logan to spend a day or two with her in Boston. In the second semester of her junior year, she sent me a paper she had written about treatments for post-traumatic stress disorder. A month later, on my way to London via Boston, I took her out to dinner at Skipjack's. I'd reserved a booth and checked ahead on the catch of the day: swordfish, her favorite.

I'd made a few notes on my copy of her paper and we talked about them, which gave me a way to ask her about her plans.

"You deserved the A."

"That guy, so tough on us, I couldn't sleep the night after I turned it in. I still can't believe he liked it." She ran her hand over the paper's title page, as if feeling it made the grade more real.

"It's good writing, as good as any I've read, Dana. Articles by pros, I mean. Have you thought about what you'll do after graduation?"

"My biology profs think I should apply to grad school—biology, or biochemistry." She wrinkled her nose.

"Why not?"

"I don't want to spend the rest of my life in a lab. Too much like practicing the piano every day." She sighed. "I want something different, that much I know."

"What about science writing?"

The corners of her mouth turned up. "Is that a real job?"

This was a family joke. I'd once overheard Grace talking to a friend about me. "She's a travel writer? That's a real job?" the friend had asked. We'd laughed about it later. But I suspected some part of Grace agreed with her friend.

I took several magazines out of my briefcase and handed them over—*Smithsonian, Discover Magazine, Scientific American.*

"I read articles in these magazines all the time, but I thought the writers had to be scientists," Dana said.

"Most have science degrees. Like the one you'll have. But they're journalists." I had brought with me the brochure about the science-writing program at MIT. "You could at least make an appointment, find out more about what's involved."

"What about Berkeley?"

Like Ben, Dana had fallen hard for Pescadero and the Bay Area. At that time, Ben, sixteen, was considering applying to the University of California at Santa Cruz, majoring in environmental studies.

"Berkeley has a good program, but it's focused on climate and the environment."

"Sounds like something Ben might like, if he doesn't get into UCSC." She flipped the MIT brochure open to the program overview. She brightened as she read. "This is more general—more sciences, plural, than science, singular. I'll check it out."

"I'm sure you can figure this out for yourself. I don't want you to feel pushed one way or the other." Especially, I didn't want Grace to think I'd tried to influence Dana's thinking. "If nothing else, a conversation with MIT will give you more information." I hoped she'd see my mentioning the MIT program for what it was: A suggestion, another option.

"Dear fellow traveler," she wrote a year later. "MIT accepted me. The only thing not on their curriculum is all the stuff that matters, like how to pack everything you need for three weeks in one carry-on. I can count on you for that part, right?"

Six years ago, when she finished her degree, I put her in touch with several editors. Since then, we've talked regularly, comparing assignments and editors, sharing gossip, mulling over story ideas, and, yes, trading tips on jet lag remedies and complaining about connections through LAX.

o o o

After the diagnosis, I battled—endured—the side effects, rode the ups and downs of hope and despair. I trusted Amy, told myself daily I was too young to die. So when Amy had declared me cancer-free, I celebrated with friends at the cabin with a weekend of hiking, fishing, windsurfing, and s'mores by the campfire. Still, months went by before I let myself believe I was healthy again.

And now, recurrence. The three R's in the word whir like a rattlesnake's rattle. Because recurrence means metastasis. This time, there's no hope. Only pain and fear.

The pain varies in intensity and location. They ask me how bad it is on a scale of one to ten. It all depends. There's no steady state. So I tell them, "Off the charts." There's a patch for the pain, which has the benefit of dulling it, distancing it. But it's still there, lurking just around the corner. That's where fear comes in: I fear the pain's return almost more than I fear death.

A nurse tells me people get over the fear.

"How?"

"They accept it."

"Give up, you mean?"

"Accept and let go."

Let go of my fear? How can I? I'm a prisoner. It's my jailer.

"Try to live in the present, Lil."

Will I? Can I? For now, I'll settle for one more sip of anticipation from the cup of joy—Dana's visit.

o o o

I wake with a knot in my belly. There, too? Now? Today? I begin to pant. Sam gets up, nuzzles my shoulder. "I'll be okay. Stay here, Sammy."

It's early. The fog hasn't yet begun to lift. Around me the milky light blurs the edges of the windowsills, my night table and lamp, the ladder-back chair beside the closet, changing the color of the Chinese kite hanging from the rafters from red to purple. From the bay, the foghorn repeats its warning, a warning dampened by the fog. I tense and relax my muscles, beginning with my feet. The knot, and my anxiety, dim.

When Amy talks to me about the progress of my disease, I cringe. This isn't the first—or the twelfth—grade, where points are awarded for progress. This isn't "my disease." I can't divorce or banish it.

How to talk to Dana about all of this? I'm apprehensive. She is, too. I can feel it. I want to go out. Have lunch at Greens. A picnic on the Headlands. A day at the cabin. We'll talk about the past, the present—her future. The arrangements I've made.

There's no time for detours.

o o o

I spend the day organizing my desk under Sam's watchful eye. He gets up to follow me every time I leave the room. What does he know? Smart as he is and intuitive, does he sense my unease?

When I finish, the stack of folders on the near end of my desk— my account information, my will, my end-of-life instructions—looks just like the stack on the far end, my ongoing-life files. I've taken special care with the end-of-life instructions because Matt will be responsible for those. We've always gotten along. I make him laugh. I imagine his expression when he opens the first file, my Last Will and Testament. I've done a good job. He'll recognize I've made his task much easier. Maybe he'll tell Grace. I'd like to think she'll recognize, at last, that I've grown up.

o o o

Coit Tower glows red gold in the sunset. I've often wondered what Lillie Coit would have made of these three nesting concrete cylinders topped by a viewing gallery. She left money for the beautification of the city, and some of it was used to design and build the tower. At the very least, she'd likely agree it is a stunning landmark.

Behind my cottage, below the verandah, in stark contrast to Coit Tower, Grace Marchant's garden of perennials, herbs, and flowering shrubs drapes the hillside next to the Filbert Steps to Sansome Street, their perfumes mingling and pooling beneath the trees. Bird calls compete with the sound of traffic rising from the street.

At six o'clock, Dana climbs the last steps to Napier Lane. Dressed in jeans and a T-shirt, a sweater slung around her shoulders, she looks sixteen, not twenty-nine. She sets her bag down on the landing just below Napier Lane and stretches.

"Need a hand?"

"Tea, please," she calls back to me.

The water is already hot. By the time she walks in, the astringent fragrance of kombucha fills the cottage. Sam prances around, panting. When we hug, my forehead brushes Dana's ear. We used to be the same height.

"What's this?" She touches the two-inch patch on my right shoulder.

"My pain patch, a.k.a. 'Pain Pal.'" I put a finger to my lips. Later. "Do you want to unpack first?"

"Then we'll talk."

"Yes."

I've made watercress sandwiches, which Dana learned to love as a little girl when we had family tea parties in Middletown. Side by side on the couch, we sip tea, eat our sandwiches.

"I have so many questions," Dana said.

"There's no rush. And I've planned some time-outs."

"Time-outs?"

"The 'fun part' of your visit, remember?"

She nods and laughs.

"Billy and I have an itinerary. I'll tell you all about it. Doom and gloom can wait."

She hugs me. "A few questions now, at least?"

I hold up three fingers.

As she asks and I answer—questions mostly about pain management and antidepressants—it's as if we're talking about someone else. It's a degree of detachment I haven't felt before. I explain about the legal work—my folders—which Matt will understand and help with, about people to call, the hospice nurses, the cancer team.

"What's wrong?" Dana leans toward me.

"Talking to you makes everything both more and less real. Normal and not normal. I mean, here we are, eating watercress sandwiches, drinking tea. Life as usual, right? Except."

"Except what?"

"The last time I got out of here was two weeks ago, for a doctor's appointment."

"Sounds like jail."

"It *is* jail. Which is why Billy and I came up with a fun plan." 'Fun' sounds like the name of a distant country.

"You don't want me to rent a car?"

"It's better if Billy drives. That way, you and I can talk and watch the world go by. No distractions. Besides, there's no telling when I'll have another chance. Or if."

"You mean…."

"I am dying." I look at her, smile at her, let my emphasis sink in. A giggle pushes up and out. Irrational. A liberation.

"Oh, Lil." Dana begins to giggle too, and we collapse together, laughing until we're sobbing, clinging to one another. Sam circles the couch, barking.

o o o

Billy arrives at eleven the next morning, hat in hand. Watching him stride down the boardwalk lane, Dana turns to me. "Still a tall, dark, and handsome devil."

At the door, Billy bends over to greet Sam, who wags and paws his knee, ignoring our laughter.

Billy and Dana hug. Dana winks at me. She leashes Sam, picks up the tote with our cameras and my pills, and opens the door.

Billy settles his hat and mimes a weight-lifter's routine, stretching his arms, shaking them out, flexing his knees, all the while watching Dana and me, a teenager's begging-for-approval grin on his face. "Right, then. Upsy-daisy!" His arm around my waist, he scoops me up. "Ninety-nine point five this week?"

"Ninety-seven point five. Don't fuss."

"A few pounds more than a month-old Jersey calf. I'll manage." Billy grins. I can't help grinning back.

I've lost three pounds in two weeks. Nothing tempts me. Not even veal parmesan, a favorite, which Billy brought me one night this week, along with a bottle of Brunello. Just to please him, I had a bite of the veal, a swallow of wine. I tasted nothing. I can't remember the last time I tasted and enjoyed a meal.

We head down the Filbert Steps, passing a black cat sunning on a bench—he and Sam ignore one another.

Billy pauses on the second landing and sets me down. "I finally figured it out, Lil." He gestures at the tree standing to our right, midway between the steps and the house above it. "It's a Tasmanian tea tree." I pointed it out one day last spring, when the tree was in bloom, its flowers about the same size as those of a dogwood, fragrant, with five petals. "The bees love it. I've got an eye out for some of the honey." He narrows his eyes, grinning, "Imported, of course."

"Save some for me."

Billy organizes Dana, Sam, and me in the back seat of his Lincoln Continental, parked on Sansome. He bought it when he decided to start moonlighting as a tour guide. Billy Best's Tours. ("That's not my last name," he told me. "But I liked how it sounds.") "Fort Mason and Greens, right, ladies?"

"And take your time."

"Still want to skip Lombard Street?" he asks.

I remember our conversation about what I didn't want to see again: Only tourists—and the people who live there, of course—go to Lombard Street, its straight 27 percent grade made crooked in the 1920s to accommodate cars.

Billy catches my headshake in the rearview mirror. "Some tourist."

Downtown, we pass through the Tenderloin. Still eye-catching, the murals, their colors and shapes, seem faded today. When I arrived in San Francisco, graffiti was the norm—erratic splashes of color, gang tags, or casual vandalism. My own experience with graffiti, my war protests, seem so innocent—and distant—now. Today the Tenderloin murals—many of them by up-and-coming local artists— loom over every street corner and vacant lot.

When the Opera House appears across the plaza in front of us, I remember the last performance I attended—*Carmen*, with José Carreras as Don José.

"And Carmen?" Dana asks.

"A complete blank, I'm afraid." That was three years ago. Amy warned me that the drugs would affect my memory. I shrugged it off, until I forgot my Napier Lane address. Now, I write everything down. When I remember.

Billy slows to a walking speed in Golden Gate Park as we drive around Stow Lake and the Japanese Tea Garden. At the entrance to the Botanical Garden, I ask him to stop and park so we can walk for a while.

I hold Billy's arm; Dana takes Sam's leash. In front of the DeYoung Museum, I spot a vacant bench and wave them on. "I'll sit here for a while."

Although San Francisco has been my home for twenty years, during the last few months I might as well have been living in Rio. Like a favela, my body has become a run-down, infested shack; my brain, foggy with chemicals, a trash heap. With Billy to drive me, I've mostly only left home to make my trips to and from the clinic, eyes closed, every mile a test of my endurance. This, my farewell tour, is a voyage of rediscovery and a homecoming.

Sam's cold nose, nuzzling my hand, wakes me. Standing in front of me, Dana looks at Billy. Billy looks down at me. "Everything okay?"

"I've been thinking about how much I love this city."

o o o

Greens, Fort Mason. I feel hungry for the first time in weeks. It's so strange to experience life's ordinary pleasures as if for the first time, renewed and precious in their novelty.

Billy and Sam leave Dana and me at the restaurant's entrance. It's crowded already, but we have a reservation, a table by the window with a view of the Golden Gate and the Marin Headlands. If only Sir Francis Drake had seen the bay on a clear day, like today, he wouldn't have turned away, wouldn't have continued north, never realizing the opportunity he missed to discover paradise on earth.

Features you know well can become so familiar that you don't see their harmony or irregularity in the present but rather as a snapshot your memory imposes on them. Today, the towers of the Golden

Gate Bridge, the cables looped between them, bright against the brilliant blue sky, thrill me anew. I see the bridge—the Marin Headlands, massed above and behind it—with all the advantages of having seen it before—a stereophonic view.

"It's always beautiful," I tell Dana. "Today, everything seems suspended in the present, timeless."

She reaches across the table for my hand.

"I'll be forty-eight in a couple of months. I'm not going to look back. Or ahead." I take her hand. "I'm here, with you, now."

"There are new clinical trials coming, you know." Her anxious frown belies the hopeful message.

"I know that. I read your article. I have five months? Six months? I'm not going to do anything that will make me feel worse." Last year, I willingly endured the pain, the hair loss, the nausea, hoping they were just hurdles, uncomfortable inconveniences, on the road to a cure, allowing myself to think about my future. No longer. Here and now. That's what I'm living for.

A ferry reaches the midpoint of its passage from Sausalito. Life as a voyage, a time-honored metaphor. Unlike the ferry's, my destination and time of arrival are unknown. I want to savor every minute that remains. "It's time like this I need for as long possible. There's so much I want to tell you."

"Is something wrong with your dessert?"

I'd ordered rhubarb cobbler with vanilla ice cream.

"Not it. Me. The meds. Everything tastes weird." I set it aside.

o o o

Billy and Sam wait for us outside Greens. Dana takes Sam's leash. When Billy picks me up, I lean my head on his left shoulder so I can look in the windows as we walk past the shops and galleries on our way to the car.

Several ceramic pieces displayed in the Earth Arts Gallery window remind me of the article I'd read about their current show, work by a potter from Lincoln, California.

"Whoa, Billy! Give me a minute." He sets me down, steadies me, and holds the door for me and takes the leash from Dana. I spot a display with a sign that reads "Funeraria."

"What are those?" Dana leans toward the pieces, each one unique, all glazed in different shades of umber and green.

"Urns," I say. "For cremains."

Dana's eyes go wide. She grabs my hand. "Remember when the flying monkeys chased Dorothy, you told me to close my eyes, count to ten, and when I opened them the scary part would be over?"

"I remember."

"I wish this were like that."

How often have I stood in a shop like this one, choosing a ceramic piece to take home in remembrance of the place I'm about to leave?

I look out the shop window. Standing on the sidewalk just outside, Billy waves. Sitting beside him, Sam focuses on the open door.

The urn had been fired in a dark green matte glaze. Nearly a foot high, with a classic, tapered shape, it holds a slender, stainless-steel cylinder. *Is there room enough?* I laugh.

"What?"

"Just enough room for a handful of dust," I tell her.

Dana looks at the urn. "Once, I asked you where heaven is. You put your hand over your heart. Then you touched mine. 'It's right here,' you told me. 'Heaven is in your heart. And mine.' That's where you'll be, Lil. Always."

Dana carries the urn. In Billy's arms once again, I reach down and pat her head.

o o o

We get back to Napier Lane a little after four. Billy takes Sam's leash from Dana. "We'll be right back."

Dana helps me undress and get into bed. She brings me a glass of water and a Tramadol. And the urn, which she places on the desk where I can see it.

"It's been a lovely day."

She kisses my forehead, her eyes closed. Outside, feathery tendrils of fog unfurl in the tree branches and dissipate in the breeze.

o o o

At nine the next morning, Dana brings me a cup of tea and a piece of toast.

"Rough night?"

"My bones ache, even ones I didn't know I have. And every pressure point feels like I'm being jabbed with a red-hot poker." I wish I could banish the worry and anxiety in her eyes. "I want to float away, like an Eskimo on an ice floe. I can't remember what it's like to feel well." Anger and self-pity surge into a sob.

Dana sits and takes my hand. "Shall I call Amy?"

"There's nothing she can do." I try to laugh. "It's a charade, really. She plays at helping me. I play at letting her think she's helping." Except for palliative care, Amy has nothing more to offer me. She can increase the dosage of the painkillers but that will knock me out. Regardless of the pain, I prefer to be awake. Then, at least, I know I'm still alive.

Isn't it written in women's DNA to bear up in the worst of times? Think of childbirth. Pain is our birthright, Eve's curse.

Out of the distant past, a memory of Grace, sobbing, pleading with me. It's a school night. I'm on my way to a party, in a miniskirt, fishnet stockings and tube top, hair teased into a helmet. Papa has already gone to bed. Grace blocks the front door. I laugh at her, taunt her, peel off my shoes, and run out the back door. I am twelve. Mama has been gone for five years. I'm so angry with them all, so angry I can't sleep. And I can't stop running.

There is some of that same anger in the way I feel now. Just like my breakthrough pain, it escapes, a wild beast shredding me from the inside out. How much longer until I can let go? Amy promised me morphine at the end. Then, I will leap into the narcotic sea that lies just below the cliff of pain mounting daily within me.

"Pain management," a phrase that appears in every cancer article I've read, sticks in my head. *"We'll take care of you. Just relax."* A marketing person who has never experienced cancer pain must have made it up. Had he, he would know that the "pain" the drug is supposed to "manage" has many levels, like the disease that causes it. "Managing" it is like trying to herd raging tigers. Or playing Whack-A-Mole. Yes. He doesn't know pain. Yes. I hope someday he will learn the hard way.

I hurt everywhere, and everywhere hurts in a different way. I'd like to believe in "pain management," but pain has made me a non-believer.

Then there's the brain fog. It has me searching for the toothbrush, lying in plain sight on the sink. And for words. For the first time in my life, I understand what it means to be at a loss for words. When I lose a word, I fall into the dark hole that yawns in front of me, right in the middle of a sentence.

Sam comes in, wagging his tail, smiling. When I don't move, he runs to the front door. I hear Billy, then Dana, but I can't make out their words.

In jeans, a red shirt, a jean jacket, and loafers, Billy kneels beside the bed. He's gotten a haircut, a buzz cut. I run my hand over it. It's as soft as one of Sam's plush toys.

He smiles. "You can 'fake it till you make it,' can't you?"

I shake my head. "These days, I'm always faking it. Today, not even that will work. You and Dana are on your own."

He sits on the floor, cross-legged, and pulls Sam into his lap. "Mom played a game with my brothers and me when we didn't want to go to school. She'd pretend to go along, all the while getting us ready, one step at a time. Pants, shirt, socks and shoes, breakfast, hair combed, teeth brushed, lunch bag, out the door. Get the picture?"

"That worked?"

"Every time."

His expression—his hope, his tenderness, his warmth—makes me want to try. "Let's see how I do."

"Atta girl." He helps me out of bed and holds my elbow until I'm steady enough to shuffle across the room to the bathroom.

Dana follows, ready to help.

As I dress, I listen in. Billy and Dana. Sitting on the couch, talking softly—about me, of course—they're already old friends. Like me, Dana knows she can count on Billy.

o o o

On the way to the Headlands in the backseat of Billy's limousine, Dana and I can talk as if we were at home, in the cottage, in the living room. For entertainment, we have San Francisco's street scenes instead of the wild parrots.

Billy takes us past Washington Square Park in North Beach.

"Have I ever told you about the time your mother and I got lost on the way to the Met?"

"When you were living in New York?"

"I'd just found an apartment in the Village and invited her to come down for a weekend. It was clear and sunny, a bit cool for September, just right for a walk. So that's what I suggested when I met her bus."

"You walked from Port Authority to the Metropolitan Museum of Art? Carrying her overnight bag?"

"It's barely three miles, Dana. And we were kids. What better way to see the city? Unless it's from the back of a Lincoln, driven by a pro."

Billy laughs with us.

"I persuaded Grace to let me be our guide for the day. She didn't notice when we turned right instead of left on Fifth Avenue. It wasn't until we got to Washington Square that she realized."

"Figured out you tricked her, you mean."

"Of course, I wanted to see the Impressionist paintings, too. More than that, I wanted Grace to see the Village. That day, there were street mimes, puppet shows, chess players, even an organ grinder in Washington Square."

"She was mad, right?"

"At first. But then she relaxed and enjoyed herself." As I knew she would.

There have been too few times like that for Grace and me.

o o o

We reach Pier 39, slowing as we near the aquarium, where Billy pulls over near a mime in a Tin Man get-up. His routine, a stop-motion enactment of the Tin Man's stiffening joints and jerky breakdown, ends in his collapse on the sidewalk near us.

"That's it. That's how I feel." I give Dana a twenty-dollar bill. "Put this in his hat, please?" As soon as the bill drops into the hat, the mime, crouched on the sidewalk, grins up at Dana and begins slowly to straighten up, one leg at a time, flexing his fingers, turning his hands, watching in wonder as his flexibility returns. The onlookers clap. Dana speaks to him, gestures toward the Lincoln. He tips his hat to me, places his right hand over his heart, blows me a kiss.

o o o

Across the Golden Gate Bridge, we take the Sausalito turn-off. The fog, lurking offshore all morning, now blankets the city. The blinking hazard lights at the top of the Transamerica Pyramid and Coit Tower transform the fog into a four-eyed monster stalking the East Bay. At the top of the access road to the Headlands, we park at Battery Spencer. The Golden Gate Bridge's towers, above the fog, stand guard over the roadway.

"Remember the time we came up here to watch the regatta, Dana?"

"That day, it looked like the fog was chasing the boats, like they were racing to get away from it."

Billy sees them first: a pair of red-tailed hawks wheeling and diving through the fog from the top of Hawk Hill behind us, plunging toward the tops of the towers, then cutting away from the bay toward the ocean.

I lean my head back and close my eyes, holding the sight of hawks soaring high and free.

○ ○ ○

Two days later, on the way to Pescadero, Sam sits between Dana and me in the backseat. At the Highway 1 exit, he lies down, his head in my lap.

I smile. "Now he knows where we're going, he can relax. The cabin's his idea of heaven."

I was awake most of last night, unable to find a comfortable spot. Now, lulled by the Lincoln's silky purr and the warm comfort of Sam's head in my lap, I lean my head against the cushion, eyes closed—not quite dozing, but almost.

"Lil, look." Dana touches my arm gently.

I turn my head to see a flock of brown pelicans heading north.

"Remember the one you rescued?"

As soon as I freed it, the bird, dazed, stumbled around, falling, then righting itself, flapping its wings as if they were foreign appendages, until it took flight at last. The whole procedure lasted less than five minutes. As it headed up the coast, we cheered. I remember the freedom I felt, the exhilaration. I long for that now.

At the turnoff to the cabin, Sam sits up, ears pricked. This is a cranky little lane, even when it's dry. Billy puts the Lincoln in low gear, centering it to avoid the brambles, easing it over the ruts.

Even through the Lincoln's thick upholstery, every bump jars my back, each vertebra signaling distress. Billy parks across the creek from the cabin. "It's pretty chilly, still. Let me get the stove going." Sam jumps over the seat and out the driver's door and races across the bridge after him.

"Ben claims that blackberry patch and your book of botanical drawings are the reasons he became a botanist," Dana tells me.

I tuck my feet up and pull my jacket around my knees. "I remember that day."

I ran back to the cabin for my loppers, leaving Dana, Tom, and Matt to comfort Ben, trapped under the blackberries.

Back at the cabin, Grace was rolling out the dough for blackberry pies. When I told her what had happened, she wouldn't look at me. "You handle it," she said, as if it were my fault, yet another example of my irresponsibility, letting a child crawl under the blackberry bushes. I wanted to stay and fight it out with her. But I had to save Ben. I grabbed my loppers and ran back to free him.

o o o

A plume of smoke rises from the chimney, drifting across the roof and into the trees. Billy sticks his head out the door. "Kettle's on. Stove's cranking. Should be warm soon."

Sam bounds out of the cabin, over the bridge to the car, and drops a pinecone at my feet. Dana picks it up and hands it to me. I look at Sam. Sam looks at me. "Just do it."

It lands six feet away—a sorry excuse for a throw. No matter. Sam bounces and hops to retrieve it, picks it up, shakes it as Dana and I cross the bridge. While waiting for the woodstove to heat up, Billy had swept and dusted, and set the table. He'd bought sandwiches and bottled water for us on the way to pick us up. He gestures at the wicker armchair. "All yours, madam." He covers me with the wool throw.

While Billy and Dana chat, I relax into the chair, giving in to "cabin time." There's nothing here to remind me that I'm ill, only objects, fragrances, and the play of light over the old floor, cocooning me in the past, the times I've spent here, working or reading, slowing down. There's a flash of light from the shelf above the bed, a piece of sea glass lying there among the pebbles, blinking at me.

"Remember the day we found the blue-green glass down by the lagoon? You told me it was more precious than gold, because it was a gift from the sea, that it had travelled miles to find us." Dana's voice catches. She laughs and rummages in her backpack. "Here it is," she says. "Still in one piece."

I hold it, eyes closed, remembering the sound of her laughter, her delight in the story I made up. For her.

o o o

After lunch, Dana and I walk upstream along the narrow dirt path. I shuffle along, stopping every few steps to catch my breath. Sam dashes back and forth, eager, but careful not to jostle me. We make it as far as the small waterfall. There's room for both of us to sit on the bank above it next to the boulder beneath a young redwood. Dana spreads the throw on the ground and supports me as I sit down on the cushion she's brought. Sam explores, snuffling in the ferns and duff, occasionally pawing the ground, whining with excitement.

Dana lies back, propped on her elbows. She looks at me. Takes a deep breath and sits up, hugging her knees. "Tell me about you and Mom."

"From the beginning?"

"You decide." She doesn't meet my eyes.

"Necessity is a cruel taskmaster, Dana. It taught Grace to suppress her own feelings—her own needs and self—to take care of me."

I tell her how I challenged Grace at every opportunity, how the more she pushed down, the more I pushed up—and out.

"If you didn't get along that well, why did she invite you to come to visit us? Didn't that seem odd?" Dana fidgets with a pinecone, frowning as she pulls off its scales.

"A little. But let's be fair. By that time, she and I had had time to grow up—apart, you know, each of us living her own life. She wasn't responsible for me anymore. When you were eight, after Papa died, you were the only family I had left. I liked the three of you. You liked me."

"And Mom?"

"We never spoke of it. But I think she was looking for a reason to invite me back into her life. Spending time with the three of you for a couple of weeks in the summer was the pretext."

Grace couldn't just invite me to visit; she had to have an excuse. The one she landed on was having me babysit while she and Matt went on vacation.

Dana hugs me. "You were more than a babysitter, Lil."

"I'm glad."

"Tom and Ben agree, you know." She pauses. Looks down. Then up at me. "Did you ever want to have children?"

"Sometimes, yes. But then, I had you, didn't I?"

"And Sam," Dana says.

Sam yawns and stands, his tail wagging gently.

She helps me up. This time, walking down the narrow path, I lean on her. She puts her arm around my waist to keep me upright.

o o o

While Dana helps Billy dry and put away dishes, and straighten the cabin, I doze on the chaise lounge on the deck, wrapped in a blanket. The sun is behind the trees now, the fog is coming in. Surrounded by trees, nestled into the rocks, the cabin resembles the cottage on Napier Lane. There, I often sit on the verandah, lulled by the sound of the traffic flowing across the Bay Bridge. Here, the gurgling of the creek and the sigh of the wind in the redwoods bring me peace.

A Steller's jay lands above me on the back of the chaise. When I tilt my head and catch its eye, it tosses its head and takes off. One black feather floats down onto my lap.

o o o

Dana has been here for two weeks. I don't want to know how much longer she'll stay. One day at a time. This morning, waves of pain in my lower back and abdomen woke me. I rolled over to get out of bed and fell on the floor. Sam nuzzled and pawed me.

I come to on the floor, a pillow under my head. Dana sits next to me beside Sam, who lies there, trembling and panting. He licks my cheek.

"Amy's on her way." Hair tousled, bathrobe askew, Dana holds a glass of water with a straw, "The hospice nurse, too. Amy said not to move until she gets here."

Broken bones? I don't know. The pain coils around me so tight, I begin to pant.

"Do you want a Tramadol? Some water?"

"I'll wait. I want to talk. Family history." I squeeze her hand. "It'll distract us both." I pull the blanket up to my chin, close my eyes, and begin. "One time, Grace was so angry, she told me she wished I would disappear. So I tried to." I open my eyes and smile.

"I overheard Mom and Dad talking about Marco once."

"She called and told me about Jean. She begged me to talk to you, to warn you."

"But you didn't."

I shift my head on the pillow to look at her. "I told her she had nothing to worry about, that she was overreacting. I told her to trust you, that if she had trusted me more, I might not have pushed so hard to escape. I told her I wouldn't interfere, anyway. My relationship with you mattered more. I didn't want to lose you. She couldn't stop talking about my fling with Marco. That's when I knew: It was as though she didn't want to give up her anger and frustration, her resentment and envy that I'd gotten away with it. It never would have occurred to you to run away, anyway—with Jean, or anyone else. I'm certain of that."

"He's become a well-known conductor." Dana shrugs.

"Of course he has."

"And we never got together."

The euphemism makes me smile. "I guessed."

"That summer, the summer I met him, I snuck out to hear his band one night when Mom and Dad were up in Boston." She shakes her head, with regret, I think. "We kissed. Twice. He held my hand, put his arm around me. Kid stuff."

"And then?"

"Just that. Except he coached me that summer. For the competition. It was like a key change in music. At least, that's how I explained it to myself."

"You were disappointed, I can tell."

"At first, I thought it was because he didn't like me in that way." She rolls her eyes. "I was crazy about him. But I was learning so much from him. The piano, my preparation, took over."

For an article I wrote years ago about space-age travel, I interviewed an astrophysicist who explained to me why warp speed is theoretically possible. What about the speed of memory, the way it can catapult you back in time to a place you'd thought you'd never see again, experiencing feelings you thought you'd never experience again?

When I ran away with Marco, Grace told me I'd ruined her life, said that Mama's death was my fault; that she wished I'd never been born.

"We got as far as Cleveland, where Marco's cousins lived."

"Mom said Mexico."

"His motorcycle died just after we crossed into Ohio. We had to hitch to Cleveland."

"So she made Mexico up?"

"It was that bad. We never talked about it."

Awareness flickers in Dana's eyes.

"After, you went your separate ways?"

"Until she was pregnant with you. I wrote to her then. She wrote back. I phoned. We talked. You gave us a way to start over."

Of course, I'd wanted Grace to admit the truth—that she was wrong to blame me for Mama's depression, for Mama's death, for giving up her childhood so I could have mine.

o o o

The monster has found my kidneys, Amy explains as she fills out the prescription for the morphine drip. My laugh sounds like a gasp. "It's just like when I had my Jeep, every time I took it to the shop."

Amy and Dana look at me, the same question in their eyes: *Have you lost it?*

"There's always something, you know?"

The hospice nurse sets up the drip and explains about the pump and the dosage. At the foot of the bed, Sam rests his chin on the mattress. His and Dana's eyes follow the nurse's every move.

"You know about lifelines, right?" I ask.

"I remember you had your palm read once, yes." Dana smiles.

"That reading didn't tell me anything I didn't already know—that the end of life is as mysterious as its beginning. Take it all in, every minute."

o o o

Dana brings me a tray set with a rose, my antique Limoges teapot and two teacups, and shortbread baked this morning. Like a trout nosing the surface of a pond, a memory swims up, nibbling at the edge of my consciousness.

"What are you thinking about?" She sets her teacup on the nightstand and leans toward me.

"A distant memory. It's the fragrances. Earl Grey tea, the rose, the shortbread. For one of my first articles for *House & Garden*, I visited a lovely old place near Oxford to interview a famous gardener. Can't remember her name. She was in her nineties, and proud of her hybrid tea roses. She called them 'spectacular.' And they were." Isabelle was her first name. It's as if she's here now, her lace handkerchief in hand, her fingernails split and roughened by weeding, her garden hat hanging over her shoulders. "How wonderful for her to visit today."

Dana leans back in the chair, sipping her tea. Birdcalls, parrot screeches and cackles, and the thwack-thwack of a helicopter mingle with the rumble of Bay Bridge traffic. Another almost-normal day. How many more?

There's a stack of printouts on the side table near my bed. "Your flight back?"

"I got a call this morning. The zoo wants me to do an article about the penguin colony." The printouts show photos of Magellanic penguins, chicks, and their burrows.

"So you get to talk to penguins for a change?"

"To their keepers, at any rate."

That this will make a positive change from writing about cancer hovers between us, unspoken.

"Since you're not going back to Boston right away, we can talk about the cottage. And a few other things."

Unlike me, she isn't ready.

"What do you mean 'talk about the cottage'? Are you going to sell it?"

I've considered different ways of telling her what I want. "I'm leaving it to you" would sound too much like I'm casting it off, like it's a used car or an item of clothing. The lawyer who prepared the papers for me several months ago commented, "This is some gift."

So it's a gift.

"I'm giving it to you, Dana." She starts to speak, but I keep going, as if I'm talking to her about something ordinary, a matter of common-sense planning. Simple, straightforward, not worth a second thought. "You have your place in Boston, of course. But, you know, maybe someday you'll want to live out here. In the meantime, you can rent it to someone. Or you could move out here and hire Billy to take care of it when you travel. You'll figure something out."

The fear in her eyes resembles the fear I once saw in a horse's eyes as the rider pushed it to jump an unfamiliar fence—fear combined with refusal. The horse and rider crashed through the fence. Both were injured.

I've removed the top rail of the fence, I think, lowered it just enough that she can make it over without panicking. She will face it. She will understand that her life will go on in a place that I love, which is a way to share my love with her, to show her that that love will last.

She swallows and shuffles the printouts in her lap. "What about Ben and Tom?"

A bit off-center, but over the fence without mishap.

"They'll have the cabin." Now teaching at UC Santa Cruz, Ben will want to live there when he can. He calls it his spirit home. He told me once that he often meditates, visualizing the creek, the pool, and the waterfall above the cabin. As for Tom, headstrong and impulsive Tom, he has channeled his energy—miraculously, it seems—into a career as a commercial airline pilot. For him, the cabin will always be the place where he learned to stalk squirrels and deer.

Dana looks at Sam, who's on the floor beside the bed, snoring softly.

"What's worrying you?" I ask.

"What about Sam?"

He lifts his head and thumps his tail.

"If I rent the cottage to someone, where will he go?"

"Back to Boston with you?"

"But this is his home too. I can't … I don't … Oh, Lil."

o o o

In the early evening, Dana helps me sit up so she can turn my pillows over. I lean against her, feeling her heartbeat.

"Mom and Dad will be here tomorrow." Her voice catches. "Billy will pick them up."

All That Remains

On the redeye to San Francisco, Matt and I had the row to ourselves. I took the window seat. Matt sat on the aisle. Once we were airborne, as soon as the seatbelt sign blinked off, he popped open the tray table, pulled out his briefcase and a bottle of water, and got to work on his latest case, a property-line dispute. Both parties had dug in, determined to see the case through. "Winning, at any cost, is the issue," Matt said. Now, he told me, a hundred-year-old deed had surfaced. Each owner claimed the deed resolved the issue in his favor, that it proved the disputed land belonged to him.

As if she were sitting next to me, I heard Lil the day I discovered the pouch tucked under her mattress. "This is *my* room, Grace. *My* stuff. Bug out!" The door slammed.

My stuff. Forty years ago, struggling to fulfill my promise to take care of Lil, I failed to recognize who Lil was. It wasn't too late to apologize, but it was past time to make amends.

When the flight attendant offered me two pillows, I stored one under the seat in front of me, tucked the other behind my shoulders, turned on the overhead light, and opened the envelope I had received from Lil that afternoon. On it, she had written "Fragile: Hand cancel." When I unfolded the letter, I understood: a 2 x 3 black-and-white photograph dropped onto my lap. Yellow and faded, the image was hazy. It was a photo of Mama holding one of us in her lap. Me or Lil? I couldn't tell. The light was too dim, the photo too faded. I slipped it back into the envelope and began to read.

9/05/10
12:30 AM

Grace,

There is so much to say, so little time. You know me and dead-lines. This one, I can't ignore. No safety net!

After all these years, Lil still submitted her articles late. Janice, her editor at *Travel & Leisure*, reserved the day before the issue went to bed to give each piece one last pass, including a fact check. Lil called Jan her "guardian angel."

Over the last couple of weeks, I've been groggy all day, sleeping on and off. The drugs, of course. Then, for reasons no one can explain, at midnight, the fog lifts. Wide awake, for a while I can think clearly. I welcome this like a cold shower on a hot day. Clear-headed at last, I can write coherent, complete sentences.

Dana keeps me company during the day, sometimes working at my desk, sometimes reading in the armchair. She brings me snacks—roasted almonds, brie and slices of apple, but I have no appetite, so I nibble. We both pretend I've eaten something. We both know there's no point in eating anything anymore.

She offered to stay up with me tonight. I declined. But I didn't tell her that I prefer to be alone for the few hours I have left, fully present in my own life.

Most of the day, I doze, unable to focus on anything except the flickering shadows on the walls and ceiling. I sometimes catch glimpses of hotels I've written about and beautifully plated meals, arrayed like paintings in a gallery or curios in an upscale gift shop. Last week Billy brought me a bottle of Châteauneuf-du-Pape, 1967, a very good year. I pretended I could taste it. He was so pleased.

By the way, if you've read about the fasting diet, trust me, it works, especially if you have cancer and your main meal of the day is a drug cocktail. Cherries Garcia tastes sweetish and sticky like that white paste we used in first grade. As for the cherries, they are just an-

noying bits you chew so you don't choke on them when you swallow. Boring. So I've lost twenty pounds. I've now hit super-model weight. (Ghoulish, I know, but that's where my humor takes me these days,)

I bet you remember Annabelle Hyatt, in your high school class, who starved herself into Vogue. We made fun of her, said she looked like she'd stepped out of "Teenage Zombies." Then we saw her Dior shoot. I'll never make Vogue, but I could probably score a spot as an extra in a remake of "Night of the Living Dead." Who said laugh so you won't cry?

The hospice nurse comes by nearly every day now. Billy, too. The nurse adjusts the meds. Billy tells me stories about his latest fares and complains as usual about his taxi's mechanical shenanigans. I know he makes up the details, but I don't let on. Sam lies on the floor, rousing himself occasionally to nuzzle or paw my hand. When I speak to him, he looks at me, intent, calm, willing me to get up and do something, anything. When his staring act doesn't work, he sighs and settles, resigned. Me, too.

I sent my last article off to Travel & Leisure *a month ago. Before that, Jan called several times to check on me. She hasn't called for several weeks.*

That's my day.

At night, I leave the window open to hear the clank of the buoy, the traffic flow on the Bay Bridge. I imagine a long-haul trucker, crossing the Bay Bridge, heading north, then east on I80, listening to country music, drinking coffee from a thermos, and looking ahead to his first stop (Salt Lake City, maybe?). A dark road on a dark night, occasional headlights flashing by, gleaming animal eyes and the indeterminate landscape, the desert, stretching into the distance. I know what that's like, now.

Sometimes, I close my eyes and visit our old house in Guilford— the fluorescent lights in the kitchen (why hasn't someone invented fluorescents that don't buzz?), the closet door in my bedroom that squeaked and stuck (why didn't someone fix it?), the door to Mama's studio, closed and locked after she died. She wasn't there when I had chickenpox, or the mumps, remember?

You got me up in the morning, ragged me about my hair and my clothes. And my behavior. That, most of all. You tried so hard to be Mama, to make me more like you. But not to be like you was who I was and who I am. I'll bet we could have been friends if we hadn't been sisters.

Did you ever wonder why we never invited friends over? Why we never had sleepovers? Once, one of my friends told me she couldn't be my friend anymore because I never invited her back.

Everyone knew Mama was dead. Every year, some new kid would ask about her and I'd have to tell the story again. I felt like a freak.

The summer before fourth grade, Emma and Sue moved in down the street, my kindred spirits. They didn't question me about Mama; they didn't pity me. They taught me how to have fun. They helped me see that family wasn't everything, that it wouldn't be long before we'd find our way to a different life.

Eventually my short attention span became an asset, as soon as I understood I was a grazer, that I had an eye for life's small change, the kind of thing that can make a good story. Until I moved to Napier Lane with Sam, I expected I'd be on the road on assignment most of the time, living out of my travel bag, moving from hotel to hotel. I learned early that what kept readers reading was often just a detail (a unique dish, created in memory of a relative, say, or the two-hundred-year-old plane tree at the center of a village square). These details give readers a sense of what it's like to live in a place they might visit one day. They can see how they, too, can live as the locals do, if only for a weekend.

Too bad no writer has come along to tell us more about what to expect when we land at our final destination. Heaven? I doubt it.

At least I don't have to pack for this trip or worry about the foreign exchange rate.

I miss the anticipation, the excitement of planning my trips, laying the groundwork, making appointments, finding the right photographer. But, out of it as I am, one of the reasons I love this little house—especially at night—is that it's like a boat, floating on the air currents that rise up the west face of Telegraph Hill and slide down the east face, here, where I used to sit at my desk writing, Sam snoring, stretched out on the floor beside my bed. Except for the desk light, the house is dark.

Often, I imagine someone across the East Bay, awake still, looking over toward Telegraph Hill, eyeing the gleam of my light, wondering about me, just as I wonder about her (or him), just as I wonder about passengers flying into SF airport, looking down at the city lights.

Hail, fellow travelers. Happy trails. Safe passage.

Remember how I used to stay up listening to my radio when Papa grounded me? Long after he locked up the house, you'd come in and tell me to turn it down. I wanted you to sit and talk to me, to tell me stories, tell me your memories of Mama.

After the funeral, I went to Mama's room and found this photograph tucked under her jewelry box on her dressing table. I thought it was me, sitting on Mama's lap. I slid it under the liner paper in my top drawer. No one would miss it or look for it, I figured. I was right: I found it there when I came home after college to pack my things for New York. Since then, I've kept it in my journal.

When I moved to Napier Lane, I got my magnifying glass and looked at it closely. That's when I noticed certain details—Mama's crooked eye tooth (right side), the small mole at the corner of her mouth (right side), the strand of hair falling across her forehead. Do you remember how she used to smooth it back and twine it into her braid?

Look at the blouse. Look at the shadow at the edge of the collar. Because the print is so old and faded, I thought the shadow was just an effect of aging. When I looked at it under a bright light, I realized the shadow is a lace border.

When I realized it's you, Grace, sitting in Mama's lap, her hands clasped around your waist, her heart beating against you, between your shoulders, I felt empty, the same way I used to feel after Mama left to go back to the clinic.

I remembered how much I wanted a blouse like that. A blouse like your blouse.

The morning she died, I found you in her room, sitting at her dressing table, looking into the mirror, crying. "Mama's gone," you told me. Later, I heard Mrs. Cullen on the phone. "Mrs. H. died this morning, Lizzie. We haven't told Lil."

Why didn't you tell me the truth, Grace?

Even after we buried her, I believed Mama would come back to us. I'd sit on the bottom stair, eyes closed, waiting for the maroon Buick from the clinic to pull up in front of the house. I imagined Mama getting out of the car, smoothing her skirt, looking up the front steps at us, smiling. Always, she wore her blue shirtwaist with the white cardigan knotted around her shoulders.

On my ninth birthday, I sat on the top step out front, waiting. She wouldn't miss my birthday, would she? I waited until Papa came home for lunch. He sat next to me, his arm around me. He didn't say a word. I smelled his pipe tobacco. Felt him breathing, slow and deep. I can't remember the weather that day. I can only remember Papa's silence, a silence that told me Mama was gone forever.

My memories of Mama faded—the sound of her voice, her laugh, the way she dried her hands, one finger at a time. Until Papa gave her dressing table away, I used to go to her room, open the top drawer, and inhale her perfume, l'Heure Bleue, until it, too, faded.

Of course, I made up stories about the picture, imagining Ma-

ma's voice in my ear, telling me about her day, about her life. I imagined her scolding me, or reminding me to wash behind my ears, or not to talk back to Mrs. Cullen.

"Mon petit choux," she called me. "My little cabbage."

When I realized it was you in the picture, I remembered the funeral. You wore the white blouse with the lace-edged Peter Pan collar, the pale blue cashmere sweater Mama gave you, and a grey pleated skirt. I wore white ankle socks, Mary Janes that pinched my toes, and the green corduroy jumper Mrs. Cullen had to shorten. The hemming ribbon she used rubbed the backs of my legs raw.

We each carried a bouquet of violets. You dropped yours into the grave. I looked over the edge. All I could see was the dark.

"Let go, Lil. Just let go," you told me. You took my hand, held it over the grave, and squeezed my wrist until I dropped the flowers. I've never forgotten the sound, barely audible, like a finger tapping a tabletop.

That's what I remember.

o o o

Midnight. Halfway there.

Eye mask in place, Matt was asleep. I switched off the overhead light and leaned back, eyes closed, considering what I knew and what I remembered, and how much Lil and I had to say to one another. Because Lil had been so weak over the last several months, she wanted me to talk when I called her. So I told her about work, about redesigning our garden, a project we had just begun. Of course, I talked about Tom and Ben. Now a TWA pilot, Tom hoped to be assigned to a route that would give him regular layovers in San Francisco, so he could spend some time with Lil at the cabin in Pescadero. Ben was teaching at UCSC. Lil and I had both laughed at Dana's enthusiasm for her latest project, an article about the penguin colony at the San

Francisco Zoo. The previous day, in the middle of our conversation, I heard the receiver hit the floor. Lil had dozed off. As soon as I hung up, I called Matt. "It's time," I told him.

o o o

While Matt collected our luggage, I called Dana, who told me Billy was on the way to pick us up.

"How is she today?"

"She was awake most of the night, but she's sleeping now." Her voice caught. "She knows you're coming today, Mom. She wants to talk to you about her letter."

When we arrived at 8:00, Dana sat on the verandah with Sam. Hair pulled back in a loose ponytail, eyes smudged with exhaustion, she huddled against me, sobbing. "This is so hard. I feel so helpless."

I held her, rocking her gently, as if she were five again, not twenty-nine. She took a deep breath and wiped her eyes. "She sometimes drifts off while she's talking, in the middle of a sentence. That's the morphine. At least she's more comfortable now."

After breakfast, I helped Dana clear and straighten up. Matt took the newspaper out to the verandah. I went into Lil's room and sat beside her bed. I had decided not to wake her. Instead, I listened to her breathing. Watching her sleep gave me an unexpected sense of peace, unexpected, I realized, because I knew the spikes of pain had become intolerable. Dana explained that she had accepted the morphine drip once Amy told how the drug would help her—keeping the pain at bay when she was conscious, so she could be fully with us. Sam, lying on the floor at the foot of the bed, came and pawed my knee. As I stroked his ears, his eyes flicked back and forth between Lil and me. "Good dog. Good Sam." He sighed and lay down beside me.

Lil turned her head toward me. She smiled. "Water, please?"

She held the water glass in both hands, sipping from the straw. I put the glass down on the nightstand and moved the chair closer to the bed. By the time I finished these arrangements, she had fallen asleep.

o o o

Sitting beside the bed that morning, I drifted on the rise and fall of Lil's breath, eyes fixed on the morphine drip, the drops forming and sliding down the tube attached to the back of her right hand.

Startled awake at noon, I looked around the room. Dana and Matt talked quietly in the living room. Now at the foot of Lil's bed, Sam snored, sometimes whimpering, softly.

Lil moaned. Holding the glass and straw in my left hand, I slid my right arm under her shoulders to lift her. She shook her head. "Talk to you," she whispered. She swallowed, cleared her throat, and leaned her head against my shoulder.

"Not my fault," she whispered.

"Not your fault?"

"Mama, dying." She shook her head. "I'm sorry. All the trouble. You tried so hard." Her lips trembled. "She never knew me, Grace. And then she died." She began to cry. "I was so angry with her. And I took it out on you."

There was so much to say, too much to say. But I had to try. I lay beside her, holding her. "Mama made me promise her to take care of you, that last time she came home." I felt Lil's nod. "I thought she meant make sure you had clean clothes for school and took your lunch every day, that you did your homework. I thought I could manage that." Lil nodded again. "I didn't know how different you were from me. You pushed away things I accepted as normal, the way things are supposed to be." Lil laughed, softly. "Instead of helping you find your way, I set up roadblocks."

"Grace ...."

"I was angry, too, Lil. It was a mystery, you know? I couldn't understand how she died, why she died. Papa told me once that Mama had lost her way. That she couldn't find her way home. After she had been in and out of the clinic all those years, he realized maybe she didn't want to come home."

"What did he mean?"

"Mama wanted to be a concert pianist. I imagine she felt torn— between us and a career in music. And when she became depressed, she gave up both. When Papa said Mama couldn't find her way home, he meant she lost hope. I think she also lost the will even to try."

"But how did she die?"

"She stopped eating. Then, heart failure."

"I was so envious, Grace."

"Of me?"

"Maybe you didn't hear, maybe you didn't know, but I heard what they said."

"Who? What did they say?"

"People said how much you looked like Mama. How you were so beautiful, just like Mama. I wanted to be just like you, just like Mama."

"But, Lil, you do look like her. The color of her hair and her eyes. The shape of her nose. I look like Papa. Those people, the ones who said I looked like Mama, they were just trying to make me feel better."

She sighed, shook her head. "I felt invisible, Grace. Like I didn't count."

o o o

Early the next morning, when the rattle began, the sound followed me onto the verandah and down into the garden. The sky was beginning to brighten.

When I came back to her, Lil was lifting and lowering her left hand, as if beating time. The rhythm of her breathing slowed; the silence between each breath lengthened. I breathed with her, falling into the silence of each pause.

At seven, Sam and I walked up to Coit Tower to watch the sunrise, leaving Dana asleep on the living room couch. Matt had left to shower and change at the hotel.

I felt it when I opened the cottage door.

Sam leaned against me, trembling, then scrambled away into Lil's room, waking Dana, who bolted up from the couch. I stepped past her into Lil's room where Sam sat, his chin next to Lil's head on the pillow. Her eyes were closed; her right arm hung down beside the bed, the hand open. Sam licked it. He looked up at me and whimpered.

Had Lil known she was alone? Had she chosen to spare us the finality of that moment?

"Lil?" Dana's voice, thick with sleep, wavered. We stood together, holding one another, sobbing.

o o o

Among her papers, Lil had left detailed instructions: *"I have an account with the Rose Funeral Home for my cremation. The process takes about a week. Please take my ashes to Pescadero and bury them next to the boulder beside the waterfall.*

"There's a carnelian from Pescadero Beach at the bottom of the urn. That's for Dana, for courage and confidence. And I want her to keep the urn in memory of our lunch at Greens the day we found it.

Grace and Matt, Billy, Ben and Ellie, Dana, and Tom—as I write this, I can see you all standing next to that beautiful little creek with Sam. Thank you for being there. Thank you for all our good times. Thank you for being you. Kisses, Lil."

Billy, Matt, Dana, Sam and I went to the funeral home to pick up Lil's urn. From there, we drove to Pescadero to meet Ben and Ellie, who were driving up from Santa Cruz. Tom, on a layover in Paris, had not been able to change his schedule. The day before, a dozen white roses had arrived at the cottage: "For Lil, with love, always, Tom."

Billy parked his Lincoln next to Ben's car, where Ellie waited for us. Ben had gone ahead to dig a hole for the maidenhair fern he had brought. As soon as Billy opened his door, Sam scrambled over the front seat and bounded across the bridge to the cabin. He scratched at the door, ran around to the back, sniffing, then darted up the path along the creek. We followed him.

Ben stood at the top of the rise with a shovel. He'd dug a foot-wide, foot-deep hole there on the bank. Sam sat, panting, next to it. Head cocked, he looked past us, expectant, then baffled. His tail thumped once. *She's not at home. She's not here. So where is she?* I crouched beside him, stroking his head.

I wondered if Sam would grieve. Would he wait for Lil in his bed beside her desk in the cottage? Billy had promised to keep him company, as he had done when Lil travelled on assignment. But that was a short-term arrangement. Would he eventually understand and accept that she wouldn't be back this time? Dana had talked about moving to San Francisco when the time was right. Maybe that time had come.

We stood in a semi-circle around the boulder. A light breeze had come up, rustling in the trees around us. Wisps of morning fog feathered the sky. The whispering creek, the play of sunlight in the water, and the call of jays and chickadees kept us company.

Holding Lil's urn and one white rose, Dana spoke. "We're here today for you, Lil, in this place you loved, to remember you. I'll always remember the time you brought me here for a 'girls only' break from work and life, and we ate vanilla ice cream and brownies for breakfast and took turns trying on make-up and sharing pipe dreams. You told me so many stories—about getting lost in the middle of the night in Sicily; about seeing Jean-Paul Belmondo in a café in Paris; about finding Sam in a basket in Béziers. All these memories and more are here with us, with you today, and always will be." She scooped some ashes from the urn, laid them in the hole, and sprinkled soil over them. She looked at me.

I'd written what I had to say. I hoped I could get through it. "One weekend, when Lil was living in Greenwich Village, I went to visit her. I wanted to see the Impressionist show at the Metropolitan Museum of Art. She wanted to show me around the Village. It was a beautiful Saturday in May. She suggested we walk rather than take a taxi.

"Lil chattered away, telling New York stories, making me laugh. When we reached Fifth Avenue, we turned right. We should have turned left, but I decided not to say anything, to wait to see what was coming.

"It didn't take long to reach Washington Square, which was crowded with artists and gallerists displaying their work, as well as musicians, acrobats, and mimes. We wandered around, people-watching, snacking on NY franks, laughing at the clowns. Occasionally we bumped into someone Lil knew.

"By four o' clock, I was ready to go to the museum. 'Too bad,' Lil said, 'It will be closed by the time we get there.'"

"I was disappointed, yes. And a little annoyed, yes. But I'd had a wonderful time with her, possibly the only time we'd ever spent together for fun.

"On my way home on the bus the next day, I thought about Lil's determination to become a writer, to travel, to see the world on her own terms. She was on her way.

"I promised Mama I'd take care of Lil. Then, I didn't realize what that meant. Or, what it didn't mean: It didn't mean that I should run Lil's life. But that's what I tried to do. That day in New York with Lil, I realized I'd have to try to let go, to let Lil be Lil. I did try. Sometimes, I succeeded. What matters is that Lil succeeded.

"Along the way, she helped Dana launch her writing career; she recognized Ben's talent and encouraged his interest in plants and botany. And Tom? Of the three of you, Tom is the most like Lil. His interests and his career grew out of his derring-do nature. Like Lil, his motto should be 'go for it.'

"Of course, I wish I'd figured all of this out long ago. Just accepting Lil as she was, as my sister, would have eased the way for us both. The night she died, we talked. We settled our differences and shared our sorrows, our lifelong sense of loss. Mama died. We lived. Talking with Lil that night, I recognized that loss was our bond. All that remains now are love and our memories. All our memories. Thank you, Lil."

Dana and Ben hugged me. Matt handed me his handkerchief.

After we'd placed Lil's ashes in the ground, Ben removed the maidenhair fern from its pot, settled it, and tamped down the soil. It would thrive here on the bank next to the waterfall, Ben had assured me. He stood, brushed off his hands, picked up his guitar, and began to play. "To everything, turn, turn, turn."

We all joined in. When we sang the final refrain, I took a rose from the bouquet Tom had sent and tossed it into the creek. One at a time, the others followed suit, and we watched the white blooms float downstream, under the bridge, past the cabin.

I closed my eyes and imagined their journey down to the river, to the lagoon, out to the sea.

Acknowledgments

Joyce Krieg dotted the 'i's' and crossed the 't's'. Patricia Hamilton (publisher, Park Place Publications) curried and combed every line. Howard Jones captured the cover photograph ("Eucalyptus," 2022 Garland Park, Carmel Valley, California). First Reader, George W. Baer helped me hear and shape the voices of Elizabeth, Grace, Lil, Matt, Dana, Tom, and Ben. I salute you all, in gratitude.